A Ghostly Suspect

A GHOSTLY SOUTHERN
MYSTERY

Book Eight

BY
TONYA KAPPES

Dedication:

This book is completely dedicated to Deborah Holt. She's an amazing reader and friend to the cozy mystery genre. There aren't enough words to even convey how much she means to authors in our genre. Deborah, we are FOREVER grateful to you!!!!

"Tell me you're a Betweener!"

The Auxiliary women rushed out of Higher Ground Café and darted across the street, *Frogger* style, with Beulah Paige leading the pack.

"Something must be wrong at the gazebo," I said to Granny and kept an eye out while everyone rushed over there.

"Come on!" Granny trotted down the steps and waved for me to follow.

No one was going to get the gossip faster than Zula Fae Raines Payne.

I shook my head, rolled my eyes, and followed behind her. I watched as the spectators reacted to whatever it was Trevor had bent over. Some of them held their hands over their mouths while others looked and then quickly looked away.

"What's going on?" Granny had sidled up to Cissie Clark and her husband.

"Dead body." Cissie gulped. Her eyes swept past Granny's shoulder and focused on me. "Emma Lee, Roger and I'll be taking our deposit back and moving our preneed arrangements to Burns."

Chapter One

"As I'm living and breathing." Debbie Dually was the last person I thought would be waiting to see me in the vestibule of Eternal Slumber. "Debbie Dually, what on earth are you doing in Sleepy Hollow?"

Debbie glanced over at the elderly couple sitting on the couch. She pulled a feather and incense from her hobo bag.

"I need to see you for just a second," she whispered as she leaned in and looked at me from underneath her blunt bangs. She tucked a strand of her chin-length bobbed brown hair behind her ear before she lit the incense.

"You probably shouldn't." I tried to stop her from lighting the smelly stick.

"It's fine." Debbie bounced on the balls of her feet, making the bell ankle bracelet come to life with happy jingling sounds.

"Mr. and Mrs. Clark, do you mind waiting one more minute?" I asked the couple, who were there to see me about preneed funeral arrangements.

Sounded creepy, but I'd found people took comfort in making their final resting place decisions and not leaving it up to their families to do. As the undertaker and owner of Eternal Slumber, I'd been able to provide these options a few years ago before any other funeral home was offering them to their clients. Now every funeral home out there offered different services, and sometimes I felt like I was behind the eight ball.

The Clarks huddled together. Mrs. Clark fanned her hand in front of her face to push away the earthy smell coming from Debbie's smoke. Mr. Clark gave her the stink eye, but Debbie didn't care. She fanned a little extra their way.

"Well, Roger does have an appointment with Doc Clyde about his gout." Mrs. Clark glanced up at her husband. Her hand was gripped in the crook of his elbow.

"Don't worry, Cissie." His wrinkled hand patted his wife's. "We've got plenty of time," he assured her.

"Do not miss that appointment." Debbie used the feather to brush more smoke over the top of the Clarks' heads and concentrated on what she saw in the smoke. "I'm not sure they have *that* much time," Debbie whispered.

"My friend has come all the way from Lexington, and she just needs one minute." I grabbed Debbie by the arm.

"If that's okay?" I asked them through gritted teeth in hopes Debbie would get the hint to cool it.

She didn't. Though she did disappear into one of the viewing rooms, probably to rid the place of any sort of spirits lingering in there.

Still, I had to make sure it was okay with the Clarks to wait a couple of more minutes, seeing how the last year I'd spent a lot of time and effort building the client list back and bringing the finances into the black for Eternal Slumber. Not that a funeral home should ever go out of business. There was plenty of business. Someone was always dying, but when they figured the undertaker was what you'd call a smidgen cuckoo, they didn't feel comfortable leaving their loved ones in my hands.

After a couple of years of being ghost-free, I felt great and back in business. Not the ghosting business. The funeral home business.

"Hello," Hettie Bell trilled when she walked into the front door of the funeral home, carrying a tray with a glass pitcher of the sweetest tea this side of the Mississippi. She set it down on the antique credenza.

Hettie stood a few inches taller than me. Her black hair was pulled into a low ponytail and her bangs were styled to

the side across her right brow line. She had on a pair of
yoga pants and a zip-up hoodie, no doubt ready to teach
one of her classes at Post and Relax, her yoga studio.

"What is that awful smell?" Hettie fanned her hand in
front of her face.

"And look here," I said to the Clarks and waved Hettie
over, hoping to avoid any more conversation about Debbie.
"You're here in time to enjoy a glass of Granny's sweet
iced tea." I smiled at the elderly couple. "Do you think you
could pour them a glass?" I winked at Hettie.

"I sure can." She pinched a smile, her nose crinkling in
an "eeww" kind of way. On her way over to pour them
some iced tea, she whispered under her breath, "But you
really need to get that smell checked out."

I smiled and sucked in a deep breath.

Offering a glass of Granny's tea was a new feature I
thought would be nice for the clients. I had coffee and
water already, but tea made people feel comfortable around
here, making it a little easier to talk about why they were
here. Let's face it, they were here about death. Either a
loved one had died, or they were anticipating the end of
one's life. Who didn't need comforting when thinking
about that?

"I have to be back to the Inn," Hettie said after she gave the Clarks their tea.

"Tell Granny hello," I told Hettie. Hettie helped out my granny, Zula Fae Raines Payne, at the Sleepy Hollow Inn when Granny needed her. "Thanks, Hettie," I called before she shut the door behind her.

"Mr. and Mrs. Clark, enjoy that tea, and I'll be with you shortly," I said to them before I motioned for Debbie to come with me to my office.

The long, flowing ankle-length chiffon material waved around Debbie as she walked.

"I'll take that," I said and grabbed the incense out of her hand, snuffing it in the potted plant on the credenza next to the tray with the tea.

Debbie nodded and slipped the feather in her bag.

"Would you like a coffee?" I asked Debbie.

"I'll take one of those teas." She looked over at the Clarks.

"Sure." I should've known. Granny's tea was well-known all over these parts of Kentucky. She always boiled her tea in the same pot, every single time. She claimed it was "seasoned." And I wasn't one to argue with her. She was the master.

"Emma Lee, your obits are late." Fluggie Callahan walked into the door of the funeral home. She was the editor in chief of the Sleepy Hollow News and here to get the list of obituaries and service times to put in this week's paper. Her dirty blond hair was pulled up in a top knot, held in place by a scrunchie. "Mr. and Mrs. Clark." Fluggie and the couple gave each other the Baptist nod.

Something I should've had done a few days ago but never got around to it.

"Good afternoon to you, too, Fluggie," I greeted her. "I'll get those to you after I finish up my meetings here."

"What's that stink?" Her white lashes were magnified under the big black-rimmed glasses she had on. She tried to find the source of the odor, her head twisting left and then right with her nose jumping up and down like a bunny rabbit. She slowly walked toward Debbie. "Hey, it's you." Fluggie made it sound as though she knew Debbie.

"Oh." Debbie turned to Fluggie. She was holding the glass pitcher of tea over the mason jar. "Have you had any luck in the…"

I shook my head, giving Debbie a hard look. The thing with Debbie, she just started to blurt out things to people she didn't know. This wouldn't go well in the very southern Baptist town of Sleepy Hollow, so I knew I had to put a stop to any further conversations and get Debbie out of here as fast as I could.

"Never mind." Debbie tipped the pitcher slightly. The orange-tinted tea poured out into the glass.

"I expect those obits later this afternoon." Fluggie gave me a hard look before she turned to leave.

"Mr. and Mrs. Clark, it'll just be a second," I assured them and ushered Debbie down the halls to my office.

Along the way, we passed an employee-gathering space along with a kitchenette where I had a refrigerator, sink, microwave, coffeepot, and a small table that was used for the four employees that worked for me. Myself included. They didn't work full-time and had other jobs.

It was also available to the families of Eternal Slumber clients during their loved ones' service.

"Let me grab a coffee, and we can go into my office." I really wasn't sure why Debbie was there, but if it'd not been for her, I'm sure I'd be in a completely different place right now.

A place with a dress code. I'm talking a white coat. Not just any white coat. The kind that wraps completely around and buckles in the back. They are very popular in places such as padded rooms.

Mmmhhhhmmmm.

A few years ago, I'd had an unfortunate accident. A run-in really. With a plastic Santa. It was Christmastime, and the entire town was all decked out for the arrival of Santa. Artie's Meat and Deli was no different. Artie had one of those big plastic Santa figures he'd put on the roof of the deli. It'd snowed for a week straight.

On that particular day, it was unseasonably warm, and the sun was shining. Since I'd been cooped up in the funeral home all day, prepping for the funeral of Ruthie Sue Payne, I'd decided to enjoy a little sunlight on my face and walk down the street to Artie's Meats and Deli to grab one of their bowls of delicious chili.

Like Granny made the best sweet tea, Artie made the best chili. My mouth was watering all the way down the street. The sun warmed my face, and there was a giddy-up in my step. Business was on a roll, and life was good.

Too good.

Before I could walk under the Artie's Meat and Deli awning, the sun had melted the snow on the roof, and next thing I knew, I heard something. I looked up, and down came that big Santa, landing right on my head, knocking me flat out.

I woke up in the hospital with more than just a knot. Literally, I thought I was a goner like the clients I'd put six feet under, because Chicken Teater, a resident of Sleepy Hollow who I'd put in the ground a few years prior, and Ruthie Sue Payne, who had been a current Eternal Slumber client, were standing right next to my hospital bed.

They were there to take me to the Big Guy in the Sky. The Maker.

Or so I thought.

When I started to talk to them, it was then that I realized I was alive, and Granny, along with Charlotte, my sister, were by my side, trying to get Doc Clyde to figure out what'd happened to my brain because I told them about Chicken and Ruthie.

It was the turning point in my life and when I realized Santa had knocked me into a world where I could see the dearly departed. Dead people.

Doc Clyde was quick to diagnose me with the Funeral Trauma. He said I'd been around the dead too long and forced Granny's hand on giving me a vacation. I'd yet to be the owner of the funeral home, so I had to do what she said because once it got around our gossipy town, clients didn't want the crazy undertaker dealing with their loved ones, and they started to cancel their preneed funeral arrangements.

Ruthie.

Ruthie was my first ghost client. Her ghost told me she was murdered. She wasn't crossing over until I helped her find her killer and bring them to justice.

Sounded easy. Not so much. Trying to sneak around and not be seen talking to a ghost had proven to be a bit harder than I'd anticipated. I thought I'd been fooling everyone and keeping the Funeral Trauma in check. Little did I know that Sheriff Jack Henry Ross was watching my every move and knew there was more than the Funeral Trauma.

He had an internal instinct that I was communicating with the dead. That's where Debbie Dually, a psychic, had come into my life.

Jack Henry took me to see her, and that's when she told me about my gift. Or a curse.

A Betweener.

"Sit down." I gestured for Debbie to sit down in front of my desk.

The sun was filtering into the old office. The wood paneling had long since needed to be replaced, but I rarely spent time in here. If I needed to see a client, I generally took them into one of the viewing rooms so they could picture what they wanted, or we went into my sister Charlotte Rae's office.

Charlotte was no longer among the living, and I missed her every day. When she came to me as a Betweener client, I didn't want to help her because I knew once I found her killer, she'd leave me... forever.

"I'll stand." Debbie's hand shook as she brought the glass of tea up to her lips. She walked over to the window and glanced out.

"How's David?" I asked about her only son. There was some tension, and she loved talking about him. Asking her about him would definitely break the ice.

"He's in his first year of college." She looked back at me and put her hand up to her mouth. "David," she gasped. Her eyes clouded with tears.

"Debbie," I got up from the chair and hurried over to her. "What's wrong? Are you okay?"

"Tell me you see dead people. Murdered dead people." A tear dripped out of her eye and down her face. "I need to hear you say it."

"Huh?" I was taken back by her unusual request. "You know I do. You've been my advisor these past few years, though I've not seen a ghost in over a year." I watched her intently. "It's been a much-needed break," I sighed.

"I need you to tell me that you see murdered people," she insisted, her voice more demanding. She turned back to the window.

"Debbie." Her serious tone made me search her face for some sort of answer. "Do you know something? Are you trying to tell me I need to know something?" I asked her.

It wouldn't be unusual to seek guidance from her and for her to tell me something about me or a Betweener client. But she's never come to Sleepy Hollow to see me or acted in this way.

"Debbie?" I put my hand on her arm.

She continued to stare outside.

"I need you to tell me you see dead people. Murdered people," she clarified, standing as still as a statue. "It's that simple. Why can't you do this for me?"

"You're scaring me." I gulped. My grip on her arm tighter.

"Don't!" She screamed and jerked away, dropping her glass and shattering it on the floor.

"Emma Lee, is everything all right in here?" Trevor O'Neil, Sleepy Hollow's new sheriff and thorn in my behind, stood at the door of my office.

He took off his cowboy hat, showing off his curly blond hair. His dimples deepened, and he moved his bright-green-eyed gaze between me and Debbie. His eyes moved down to the broken glass.

"It's fine." I hurried into my bathroom and grabbed a towel.

What on earth was he doing here? My thoughts made my stomach gurgle. Ever since Trevor had been named Sheriff, replacing Jack Henry when he left to take a position at the Kentucky State Police, he'd made my life a living hell.

Literally.

"Miss?" I heard Trevor refer to Debbie.

"I'm fine," I heard her whisper, followed up by fast footsteps.

I came back with a towel to clean up the mess when I noticed Trevor and I were all alone.

"Where did she go?" I asked him, narrowing my eyes. "What did you say to her?" I bent down and picked up the larger pieces of glass, piling them up before I used the towel to start sopping up the tea.

"Maybe I should be asking what you said to her to make her yell at you and why you had a hand on her." He took slow steps toward me and stopped as he towered over my hunched body.

"What do you want?" I asked him and stood up. "You sick and need some arrangements? If you do, I hear Burns Funeral has plenty of openings."

I might've been a little cruel saying such a thing to him, since I didn't wish harm or death on anyone, but he didn't make my life any easier around here. Plus, I did take some pleasure in the low client rate Burns Funeral, the other funeral home in Sleepy Hollow, was having at the moment.

Trust me, Bea Allen Burns swooped up in here when her brother, O'Dell Burns, was elected mayor, leaving Burns Funeral in need of another director. It just so happened to be the time everyone was looking for a new funeral home due to the Funeral Trauma diagnosis. Bea Allen did everything she could to steal my clients, and she did.

Now it was my turn.

"I'm not going to give you another warning. This is it." Trevor took a fistful of papers out of his brown sheriff-pants pockets. "Here are copies of the parking tickets you owe. I just gave you another one today. You can't park your hearse anywhere you feel like when you're not picking up a body. I don't understand why you think you can park in a yellow zone, Emma Lee."

He extended the pile of yellow citations at me.

"What makes you think you are above the law? You've given me fits since my first day on the job, and it's going to stop." He jabbed his hand toward me again.

I was reluctant to take them.

"This is your last warning." When I didn't take the tickets, he walked over to my desk and threw them in the air like confetti. "You have until the end of the week to pay all of them, or I'm going to arrest you. I'm not joking." He shoved the hat back on his head. His brows wiggled, and he smiled, his dimples deepening. "Have a good day." He stuck the cowboy hat back on top of his head.

Chapter Two

Sleepy Hollow was a cave-and-cavern town in Kentucky that was deep in a hollow. Eternal Slumber was downtown along with most of the other businesses. Residents lived around the town, but the town square was where all the action took place.

The town square was exactly that. A square. There was a grassy park in the middle of downtown where everyone gathered. There was a big gazebo that was perfect for all the events we did as a community. Four roads ran alongside the town square with Main Street being the facing road.

Eternal Slumber was located on the right side of the square along with Pose and Relax, a yoga studio that was owned by Hettie Bell. It was Hettie's real job, and she only worked for Granny at the Inn part-time when she didn't have classes scheduled at the studio.

Girl's Best Friend Spa, Artie's Meats and Deli, the courthouse, Higher Ground Café, and Doc Clyde's office were all located on Main Street, which was directly in front of the square. A little further down on Main was where the

Normal Baptist Church was located and where you could find the entire town on Sunday mornings.

Directly across from the square opposite from Eternal Slumber was the Sleepy Hollow Inn and Antiques. That was Granny's place. More an inn than an antiques store, since she'd converted the actual shop into another dining room once she'd taken over the Inn fully after Ruthie Sue Payne had died. Long story. Granny did use some of the antiques as decorations and had price tags dangling off them, but since her renovation to bring the Inn up to date, she'd gotten away from adding any more antiques.

Antiques were not the reason tourists came to town. It was the caves and caverns.

On the opposite of Main Street and the road behind the square, there was a cemetery and a trailer park. It was nice having the cemetery close to the funeral home. This week I was going to be very thankful for the closeness because for the funeral I had scheduled for tomorrow, the family wanted to walk the casket to the cemetery for a graveside funeral. And a little further away from the square was where Burns Funeral Home was located.

You wouldn't believe the strange requests I'd get as an undertaker. Not from the Clarks. During our meeting, they wanted the typical day-before layout and visitation with a next day follow-up funeral. I was so happy Debbie hadn't scared them off.

Not that Debbie wasn't an amazing person, but around these parts, people didn't like to think of psychics or possible spirits running around. That's why I was happy I'd been ghost-free for a while.

"I see dead people," I harrumphed and opened the door to the Higher Ground Café to get my late afternoon cup of coffee before I walked over to the Inn to check on Granny today.

After visiting with Granny, I'd give Debbie a call and see if she'd settled down from earlier in the afternoon when she'd stopped by and abruptly ran out.

"Shhh. There she is." I heard the murmur of my arrival from the table on the left. When I looked, it was no surprise to see members of the Auxiliary group with their heads together. Beulah Paige Bellefry, Mable Claire, Marla Marie Teater, Mazie Watkins, and Cheryl Lynn Doyle all looked up, as innocent as could be. All eyes were on me, with fake grins planted on all of their faces.

"Let's get it out into the open," I told the group of women who had more gossip between them than all the people employed by one of those national gossip magazines. "Here I am. What's going on?"

"It's nothing." Cheryl Lynn, owner of Higher Ground Café, jumped up and scooted me through her café to the counter. "It's just that we heard about that weirdo moving into Sleepy Hollow. Some of the gals," she started to say, leaning her head to the side, her eyes sweeping past my shoulder. I turned to look and saw the other ladies encouraging her to say something. "Well, the other gals don't think the psychic kind needs to be here in Sleepy Hollow. They've done gone to Pastor Brown about it, Emma," she whined with concern. "I even think the Baptist church is going to hold a meeting about that kind moving in here."

"Debbie Dually?" I snorted. "They think Debbie is moving to Sleepy Hollow?" I asked and laughed louder. "Wooooo, wooooooo." My voice shook with fright along with my hands shaking in the air as I tried to be all spooky. "Don't worry, y'all," I turned around to inform them. "Not that it matters, but Debbie Dually isn't moving here. No way. No how."

"Then why was she here, and why did she do that voodoo stuff in the funeral home?" Beulah Paige asked, tossing her long salt-and-pepper hair behind her shoulder. Her blue eyes focused on me.

Beulah Paige was the leader of the pack and the Auxiliary women's club president. She had spent a lot of time trying to stay young with her fake lashes and her fake tan, all of which she denied, though she did stay in great shape for forty-five.

"Not that I need to explain anything to you," I directed my comment at her when I walked back over to the counter to wait for my iced coffee. "Debbie is a friend of mine, and I didn't realize it was against the law for a friend to come visit."

"Something was against the law because Fluggie said Sheriff O'Neil also stopped by on some business he had directly with you." Beulah Paige was also the CEO of gossip in Sleepy Hollow.

"Did she?" I asked and remembered I needed to get the obits over to her. Fluggie must've passed Sheriff O'Neil on her way out of the funeral home. "And it's your business why?"

"How's Zula?" Mable Claire spoke up. She dug into her pocket and took out a couple of coins, handing them to the two little kids who passed by us. It was something she'd done ever since I knew her. She loved giving money to kids. "I've been meaning to stop by and see her. I know she's still having a hard time with Charlotte Rae and the wedding. Every time I ring her to do something, she's always got an excuse."

Mable Claire and Granny were best friends, and I didn't want to see Granny become a recluse, so I wanted to make sure I stopped by the Inn to check on her.

Granny was having a hard time? We'd never get over Charlotte Rae's death, but we dealt with it. The wedding, well, it was a whole different story.

Granny and Doc Clyde had been engaged, and she'd even tried on several dresses. White ones. After they'd gotten engaged, they'd started spending a lot of time together. More than their casual get-togethers. Doc Clyde loved Granny and everything about her, almost becoming too needy of her. Granny, on the other hand, came to the realization that she didn't want a traditional husband. She only wanted a companion when she wanted one, not when he wanted one, which was all the time, all day long. So much so, he wanted to retire and wanted her to retire.

Granny wasn't about to give up her Inn or her freedom, leaving Doc Clyde's ring on the patient table in his office.

It wasn't without a note from her. She wrote a Dear John letter on the white paper that Ina Nell, Doc's receptionist, put on the patient tables for protection.

Needless to say, Doc Clyde and Granny haven't spoken in a year.

"She's doing fine. In fact, I've got to get going because I'm heading over there right now to get more of her delicious sweet tea for the clients at Eternal Slumber." I gave each one of the women eye contact before letting my stare linger on Beulah. "I'll make sure to tell her that you asked about her."

She shifted in her seat and looked away from me.

"Whoever heard the likes," I overheard Beulah whisper to the ladies since she always wanted to get in the last word in edgewise. "Offering iced tea when people are grieving. The last place they want to sit and chat is a funeral home. The repast, yes, but not while making arrangements."

I stopped, swiveled around on the soles of my shoes.

"What was that?" I looked into the air like I could hear someone they couldn't see. You know... stir the Funeral Trauma pot a little, just to keep Beulah on her toes. "Beulah? Really?" I laughed and slide my gaze to her.

All the Auxiliary women drew back, lightly gasping.

"Do you think she's got the trauma again?" Beulah planted the seed in their heads on my way out the door.

"Noooo." I didn't have to look back when I heard Mazie respond.

I'd be getting a visit from her soon now that Beulah had planted that little seed of doubt in her mind.

Chapter Three

It was a beautiful sunny day, and sitting in one of the rocking chairs on the covered front porch of the Inn while visiting Granny was exactly what I needed to calm my nerves from Beulah Paige and the gossip she'd already started to spread about me.

"Don't you pay her any attention." Granny _tsk_ed. "That woman talks enough for four sets of teeth."

Granny used the toe of her shoe to push the rocking chair back and forth.

"You doing okay?" I glanced over at her.

For nearly eighty years old, Granny was still very spry. She kept her hair short and dyed to a bright red. She dressed to the nines and always was a southern lady. Even when she blessed your heart through gritted teeth. Granny knew exactly how to make someone feel at home but stab them in the back if she needed to, and they'd never see it coming.

"I'm good." She nodded, her stare straight across the town square. "I've got a meat loaf in for the repast tomorrow. I even made an extra one for you and Jack

Henry." There was a glimmer of hope in her eye that told me she'd wished I was married, because to her, I was considered an old maid. "It's date night, ain't it?"

"It is. And he's going to love the meat loaf." My mouth watered at the thought of her recipe.

I wasn't about to turn away Granny's specialty. Heck, everything she made was special.

Her meat loaf was made with two different types of meat, and it was always moist as well as tasty.

"You tell him you made it. That'll get him back here." She winked, still trying to get me to the altar.

"When you get married, I'll get married." It was all I had to say to shut her up. "By the way, the clients love your tea."

"Hettie Bell told me." Granny gave me the side-eye. "Emma Lee, you feeling all right? Hettie told me some woman was at the funeral home waving a feather around like it was some sort of voodoo spirit stuff. And we aren't going to Doc Clyde this time. I'm getting you a real doctor."

Until Granny and Doc Clyde had split up, Doc Clyde, in Granny's eyes, was as close to a Godly man on earth as you could get, outside of Pastor Brown. She'd obviously changed her mind when she decided not to marry him.

"Everything is good. I'm not ill." I assured her and looked at my new fancy watch when a text chirped from it.

"I dee-clare." Granny pushed herself up to stand. "It was cell phones that took all our attention. Now you have that watch. Can't you just sit a spell and not be disturbed?"

"It's Jack Henry." I read his text, telling me what time he was coming tonight.

"As long as it's him." Granny had a twinkle of hope in her eye. "In my day if you were near thirty…" she reminded me as she got up.

"It's not your day." I raised my brows and in a nonchalant way told her it was none of her business. "We are fine. Happy and good."

"When's he coming back to Sleepy Hollow to take over as sheriff again? I'm tired of Trevor." She walked down the porch and picked the dead leaves out of the potted ferns, tossing them over the railing of the porch.

"You're tired of Trevor? I'm sick to death of him." I'd forgotten about his little visit this morning and knew I needed to take care of my little citations. "He had the nerve to bring me all the parking tickets he's given my hearse over the past couple of years and told me that he was going to arrest me if I didn't pay them."

The sounds of sirens bounced off the mountains behind the Inn and echoed through the town square.

Granny and I met at the top step of the porch and looked around to see what was going on. There were a few people gathered near the gazebo. The sirens got louder and louder.

"Maybe Trevor is coming to get you now," Granny joked when the sheriff's car skidded into the parking lot across from the Inn.

The Auxiliary women rushed out of Higher Ground Café and darted across the street, *Frogger* style, with Beulah Paige leading the pack.

"Something must be wrong at the gazebo," I said to Granny and kept an eye out while everyone rushed over there.

"Come on!" Granny trotted down the steps and waved for me to follow.

No one was going to get the gossip faster than Zula Fae Raines Payne.

I shook my head, rolled my eyes, and followed behind her. I watched as the spectators reacted to whatever it was

Trevor had bent over. Some of them held their hands over their mouths while others looked and then quickly looked away.

"What's going on?" Granny had sidled up to Cissie Clark and her husband.

"Dead body." Cissie gulped. Her eyes swept past Granny's shoulder and focused on me. "Emma Lee, Roger and I'll be taking our deposit back and moving our preneed arrangements to Burns."

"Why on God's green earth would you do something so silly?" Granny was quick to come to my defense.

"By the looks of it…" Cissie slid her gaze back to Trevor. "Emma Lee is gonna be gone for a long time with no one to run Eternal Slumber."

"What?" My brows furrowed. A nervous laugh escaped me.

"Oh no, Emma." I turned away from Cissie and looked at Debbie Dually, who was standing right next to me.

"Where did you go earlier?" I asked Debbie and noticed she looked a little pale after some of the smoke cleared from around her. I fanned my hand in front of my face, "You've got to put that incense out," I whispered.

"Here." Debbie pointed to the gazebo. "I came here."

"Clark and I picked up a lunch at Artie's and then came here to eat it." Cissie, for some reason, was answering my questions I had for Debbie.

I didn't want to know where they'd gone. I wanted to know where Debbie had disappeared to after she dropped the tea glass in my office.

Cissie Clark nodded to the gazebo. Trevor O'Neil stood up, and the crowd parted as they followed his eyes and what he was fixated on.

Me.

For a split second, I stared back before my focus dropped to his feet and Debbie Dually lying on the ground. Her eyes were open. Smoke was coming from the incense still burning in her hand. There was an empty mason jar with a little bit of tea in the bottom. It sure did look like one of the mason jars I served Granny's sweet tea in at Eternal Slumber.

I jerked around and looked at Debbie Dually, who was standing next to me.

"But…" I stammered when the ghost of Debbie was clearly by my side. "Is this why you came to see me?" I tried to blink back all the confusion.

"Emma Lee." Granny tugged on my arm. "What are you doing? Hide that crazy. Tuck it up inside of you right now."

"I need your help." Debbie Dually's ghost looked frightened. "I saw my own death before I was killed."

"Killed?" I gulped.

Chapter Four

Granny had dragged me back over to the Inn along with the Auxiliary women. She was busy serving tea and cookies while I was sitting on the top step watching the sheriff's department assess the murder scene and scour the funeral home. Trevor said he'd get a warrant if I didn't let them go through Eternal Slumber since he had enough evidence to get a judge to grant one.

Trevor said, "I'm not saying this is a murder, but it's strange to me that I heard you and Debbie Dually had a loud conversation for the Clarks to think you two were fighting, not to mention when I walked into your office you had your hand on her before she dropped her glass. Now she's dead?"

I had nothing to hide. I knew she'd been murdered, but it wasn't like I could tell him. I didn't kill her, and I wanted them to find out who did do it.

"Fine," I told him. "Do whatever you need to do in the funeral home." Here I sat. Watching from clear across the town square, trying to figure out why on earth someone would want Debbie dead.

I kept an eye out for Debbie's ghost, but she seemed to disappear. The only thing I could recall from Debbie's visit this morning was the fact she wanted me to tell her I still saw dead people.

I saw my own death before I was killed. Debbie's words played over and over in my head. What did that mean? Who on earth would want Debbie dead? Why was she killed in Sleepy Hollow? If she saw her own death, didn't she know who murdered her? These were all questions I was eager to ask her.

"Emma," Mazie whispered and sat down on the step next to me. "Is she?" Mazie jerked her head to the right in two quick motions as if she were gesturing to someone. She didn't bother finishing her sentence because I knew she meant the ghost of Debbie Dually.

"Not at this particular moment," I muttered, nervously glancing over at Mazie.

"It's been a while." She reminded me of the last Betweener client I had and how she pegged me as a Betweener after I'd gone to the library to do some research.

Mazie Watkins was the librarian. She knew something was up when I'd come to the library a few times in a week and during a case with a Betweener client. Not only that, but I also didn't know how closely she'd been watching me over the previous years after I was diagnosed with the Funeral Trauma.

Bogus diagnosis, she'd said. She was very well-read in all genres and topics, including the paranormal. When she noticed how I would cover things up and that when I did do research, it was only when people were murdered, she started to research my actions and how I thought I was sleuthing… undercover.

During my last Betweener case, Jack Henry had decided to take the Kentucky State Police job, leaving me here alone with my secret.

It felt like a ton of bricks hit me when Mazie had confessed how she'd been watching me, recording my every move in her head, and knew I was able to see as well as communicate with dead people. When I confessed to her it was specifically murdered people, she was beyond thrilled and instantly insisted on helping me. She convinced me that she had skills in finding things out that I couldn't with her access to different databases and that she could help out tremendously when I was involved in a Betweener case.

"Shhhh." Mazie nudged me and nodded over at the square.

Trevor O'Neil was walking over to the Inn. His cowboy hat was tucked up under his armpit. A sigh of relief swept over me when he stopped to put his hat in his sheriff's car.

"Crap," I groaned when I realized he'd just made a pit stop and continued his journey over to the Inn.

"Keep your cool," Mazie instructed me like she'd been through this a million times with me. "What was her name, and how did you know her?"

"What?" I asked her.

"What's the woman's name? I'll go get started doing... you know," she said in a mysterious tone, her chin slowly turned toward me, her head tilted down.

"Debbie Dually. Psychic from Lexington who told me I was a Betweener." The words quickly rolled out of my mouth just in enough time for Trevor not to hear me.

"Hi, Trevor," Mazie gushed and jumped to her feet. She tucked in a strand of her chin-length short, wavy brown hair behind one ear and swayed a little to the left and right.

She loved to flirt with Trevor. The first day we'd seen him was when we were in Southern Comfort, a clothing boutique, waiting for Granny to try on a dress suitable for her wedding. It was the first ticket I'd gotten from him, and it certainly wasn't the last.

"Ms. Watkins." The smile he always gave Mazie never went unnoticed. "It's good to see you, but I'm here to talk to Emma Lee."

"No. I haven't paid the tickets yet." I stuck my wrists out. "Just arrest me."

"Arrest you for the tickets or the murder of Debbie Dually?" he asked.

"Murder?" Mazie laughed nervously. "Trevor, you've got to be kidding? I just saw Emma Lee at Higher Ground Café, and so did…"

The screen door to the Inn creaked opened. Without turning around, I knew it was Granny, closely followed by Mable Claire, the rattling change giving her away. They came out to the porch to see what was going on.

"Murdered?" Granny gasped.

"There aren't visible signs of the cause of death, so we will wait to see what Vernon Baxter says." The sound of the rolling gurney came from the square, making us all look. Vernon Baxter didn't have to go far to get the body since he worked at Eternal Slumber, and the county morgue was in my basement. "Emma Lee said murder, Mrs. Payne, not me. Unless Emma needs to get something off her chest." Trevor looked back at me like he'd already convicted me.

"Look at her, Trevor." Mazie rotated to me and put her hand out. "You can see she's upset. Her friend is dead."

"I'd be ashamed, Trevor O'Neil." Granny was going to shame Trevor right off the Inn's steps. "You coming here like this and accusing Emma Lee of such a crime. If you're going to arrest her, get on with it so I can get a lawyer down there to get her out on such bogus charges. And you don't even know if she was murdered."

"Ma'am, I didn't say I was going to arrest anyone, but I would like it if Emma would come down to the station and answer a few questions I have for her." He was going to start the investigation with me, and it was for a good reason. "Just formality. To help out her friend and all." The sarcasm poured out of him.

"Is that…" Granny started to say. I stuck my hand out behind my back to have her stop talking.

"It's fine. I have nothing to hide." I stood up. "I'm more than happy to meet you down there. Now?"

"No time like the present." Trevor looked pleased with my willingness to go and not be coerced. "Ladies." He nodded Granny's way and at the other women. He shifted his eyes to Mazie. "Ms. Watkins."

"Trevor." Mazie's voice was flat.

Trevor turned and walked back to his car. I gave us a minute to watch him and let him get in before I addressed the women behind me.

"This is ridiculous," Mazie spat.

"Ridiculous or not, Debbie did come to see me this morning, and now she's dead." I glanced over to the square.

Cissie and Roger Clark were still talking to an officer near the gazebo. It looked as though they were giving him a statement. Cissie lifted her hand and pointed my way. Roger and the officer looked. Roger said something, and the officer went back to writing something on his pad of paper.

I gnawed on my lip and walked down the steps. I turned around and looked at Granny. "Don't worry. I'll be back in time to get that meat loaf."

"You're not going alone." Mazie hurried along beside me down the sidewalk of the square.

I wasn't about to walk through the square and around the police line. It was the last place I wanted to be. Especially since Vernon Baxter was rolling Debbie's body across the square so he could take her to the morgue.

It might've been a conflict of interest for me to have Debbie in the basement of my place of employment and where I lived, but maybe it was a good thing too. Vernon would have all her death records there, and Vernon would surely tell me how she was murdered before he let Trevor know it was changed to a homicide. There was a little window of time for me to get a jump on who might've done this heinous act.

"You don't need to go with me. They aren't going to arrest me. They don't even know that she's been murdered. Only we do," I said over my shoulder to Mazie. "What I really need you to do is to find out any information you can find on Debbie while I'm down there giving my statement."

It seemed like a great place to start.

"I do think she knew that she was going to be murdered, and I didn't stop it." I stopped in front of the funeral home.

"Why do you think that?" she asked. She blinked with confusion.

"Debbie didn't have an appointment with me, and she came in all nervous, waving a feather and incense around like she was warding off something." I proceeded up the steps and walked into Eternal Slumber. Now I wished I'd asked her why she was burning the incense. Hindsight. "She insisted on me telling her that I still saw dead people. The Clarks saw it all."

I stopped at the credenza, where Granny's tray with her glass pitcher of sweet tea was sitting, and counted the mason jars. I had eight, and there were only five there.

"I thought you said she was the one who told you about your gift." Mazie halted and watched me count and recount.

"She did. For some reason she wanted me to confirm it out loud, and I wasn't sure why until now." My body stiffened in shock when I realized just why she did insist. My eyes darted nervously back and forth as I put the scenario in my head into words. "She saw her death coming. I bet she knew I'd not seen any Betweener clients for a while and wanted me to confirm so she could become my client."

"Say it," the ghost of Debbie Dually appeared.

"I can see and hear you. I promise. Just like I saw you over there." I walked over to the door and looked back over at the gazebo.

"She's here?" Mazie's eyes widened in alarm. "Hi, I'm Mazie, and I'm going to help Emma."

"We've got an eager one," Debbie joked and ghosted behind me when I headed toward my office, where I needed to grab my purse and keys so I could hurry up and get this over with.

"How was she murdered?" Mazie was digging right on in and followed behind Debbie, though she had no idea Debbie was in front of her.

"And she gets right down to it too." Debbie ghosted up to Mazie and surveyed her kindly. "Tell her I don't know. If I knew that and who did it, I'd have already told you."

"She said she has no idea who and how she was murdered." It was the beginning of the investigation, and it didn't look good for me since there didn't appear to be any visible signs of murder, which made me think of poison or something internal. "All I know is that I have a few people who saw me with you this morning and how you had a glass of tea at the crime scene."

"The cop did put that in an evidence bag," Mazie said. "Then I saw them interviewing the Clarks."

"I'm sorry, Emma Lee." Debbie's eyes traveled down to her feet. "I didn't know I was going to be murdered in Sleepy Hollow, so I'm going to need you to go to my house. I'd asked David to come home from college a week early. He even got permission from his professors to take his exams early."

"You want me to tell him that you're dead?" I blinked rapidly at her, before I turned to go back into the vestibule.

"He knows you." Debbie said quietly but with emphasis from behind me. "He needs to hear it from you. I thought I had a few days. I was wrong."

"What is she saying?" Mazie asked, continuing to follow me around.

"Her son is coming home from college today, and she wants me to go there and tell him before I go to the police station." I knew how the cops worked. They'd get all her information and tell the next of kin, which would be David. They'd have to spend the time to try to find out where she lived along with getting that information about David. It was a good step that I could just skim right over.

"You have to." Mazie answered in a rush of words. "He has to hear it from you and not one of them." She gave a quick lift of the chin to the cops gathered in the square. "Trevor can wait a couple of hours. You told him you'd be there. You didn't give a time."

"Okay." I had a pit in my stomach telling me that I might just regret agreeing to the new plan of driving to Lexington to tell David then stop by the police station on my way back into Sleepy Hollow. Then I suggested, "I'll head to Lexington after I go give my statement to Trevor."

"No. You have to go now," Debbie's ghost insisted. "They might beat you there. There's not any time to spare. Now, Emma. Now."

"But—" My voice broke off in midsentence when I realized Debbie had ghosted away.

"But what?" Mazie asked. "I don't like being out of the conversation."

"There's a whole lot I don't like about the conversation, but this is how this works." I gestured between me and Mazie. "I talk to the ghosts. You do the research. She said I have to go tell David now and go give my statement afterwards."

Mazie gnawed on her bottom lip. Her brows furrowed. "You've got to do what Debbie says since she needs your help, but Trevor can put you in jail for not coming."

We stood at the front door of Eternal Slumber and looked across the street.

"Trevor can't do squat without opening the case up as a homicide, and right now, it's not." I sucked in a deep breath to try to make the knot in my stomach go away. There was something not sitting well with what Debbie wanted me to do. "I'm on borrowed time."

I gulped when I saw the Clarks were still in the square talking to town folks about what was going on and what I had to do with it because all of them turned and stared right at me.

Chapter Five

The entire forty-minute drive to Lexington was spent going over everything that'd happened from the time Debbie Dually had shown up at Eternal Slumber until she ghosted away when I left to drive up here to her house.

I'd thought Debbie might make an appearance and at least give me an opportunity to ask her some specific questions. I'd like to know who might have had something against her to do such a thing or even if she had friends that I could talk to. In reality, I had never been a good friend like she'd been to me. In all honesty, I never even looked at Debbie as a friend. More as a mentor who helped me figure out what my purpose in life was, something I'd obviously not chosen.

When I'd go see her, I'd dump all my issues on her about my Betweener clients and how I was going to help them, seeking her advice. Rarely had I asked about how she was doing, though we did talk about David.

Oh, David.

A million different scenarios bounced around in my head on my drive from Sleepy Hollow to Lexington on how

I'd tell him about the fate of his mother. I also had decided to bring David back to Sleepy Hollow with me for the night so we could try to figure things out. How safe was Debbie's house if she knew someone was going to kill her?

They had to have known she lived in Lexington and had followed her to Sleepy Hollow, where she'd met her untimely demise.

Before I knew it, I had pulled up in front of her small brick home and knew exactly what I was going to say to David. So much so, I could already see the look on his face and how I'd respond to his reaction.

I grabbed my crossbody from the passenger side and got out of the hearse, throwing my keys inside my bag as I placed it over my shoulder. I was relieved when I noticed there wasn't a car in her driveway. I'd beat David home.

"The key is under the fairy near the mailbox," Debbie's ghost called out to me. She was seated on the one step leading up to the small porch of her house.

I smiled at her. I was thankful she was here for when David got home. Once inside and out of any eyes of prying neighbors, I'd question her once we were alone.

"Ma'am! Ma'am! Are you Debbie?" A young woman was standing by a beat-up blue car that had more rust than paint. Her blond hair was braided all over her head, and some was knotted up in dreadlocks. "I know I'm late for our five o'clock appointment, but I had to work late. Another server was late for her shift and, well." She stood in front of me. She smelled of greasy fried food, and it was oddly pleasing to me. She pushed back her hair, and I noticed her fingernails were so short that she had to be a biter. "Like I said on the phone, I just need some clarification."

"Invite her in," Debbie urged me and swept near the girl. "She's in need, and we can help her."

I jerked around and stared at Debbie with wide eyes.

"She's here, isn't she." The young girl put her pointer finger in her mouth and started to gnaw on what little nail she had left. "I knew it." She smiled with a look of relief on her face.

"Jody. Her name is Jody. Invite her in," Debbie was insistent.

My phone chirped a text deep in my bag.

"I really need to ask her something. Please. I'll still pay for the full hour," she pleaded.

I let out a long sigh and took my phone out to buy me some time to think about if I should tell Jody to go or do what Debbie had wanted me to do.

"It'll be all fine, Emma Lee." Debbie's soft-spoken voice had always appealed to me. It was one thing that made me feel comfortable in her presence. I should've known when she was talking so fast and insistently earlier this afternoon when she wanted me to confirm my gift. "I'll guide you."

I looked down at my phone and saw there was a text from Jack Henry.

What is going on down there? I heard on the scanner there was someone dead in the square. Who is it?

"Emma." Debbie caught my attention. "She's waiting."

I glanced up and looked at her, but she wasn't alone. There was another ghost standing next to her, only she was more of a light and less of a form, like the rest of my clients. There was no definition to the form. I could see it was a woman but not her eyes or even what she was wearing.

"Don't worry." Debbie must've seen the look on my face. "She's not murdered. These are my clients."

Debbie lifted her hands in the air, and when she did, it was like lifting a veil away from my eyes, and all sorts of wispy ghosts were moving about her property.

"This is what I see. Souls who want to connect with family and friends. Jody is here to connect with her grandmother. She's looking for the brooch. Her grandmother's brooch. According to her grandmother—" Debbie started to say but was interrupted in midsentence by the figure.

"Jody sold my brooch. I just couldn't believe it. It's worth a lot of money. She lost her mind and sold it when she was dating this guy who needed some money. I didn't trust him and haunted him until he finally broke it off with her." The elderly woman's features started to come into focus the more she talked to me.

"The grandmother is ready to tell Jody about the brooch. Jody needs to get the brooch for the family. That's why you need to pretend to be me for just a few minutes. That's all," Debbie said and looked at the fairy statue. "The key."

I gulped, decided to text Jack Henry back after this little stunt of pretending to be Debbie, and stalked over to the mailbox to retrieve the key from underneath the fairy.

"Just a quick minute since you're late." I didn't confirm Jody's suspicions about how her grandmother was there.

With the key in my hand and Jody on my heels, along with Debbie floating beside me, I unlocked the door and stepped inside.

"Turn the light on by the chain." Debbie and the grandmother ghost had moved into the room on the right. It was where Debbie always took me when I came to see her. "Tell her to wait next to the door."

"Wait by the door, please," I told Jody and added a little bit of southern manners. "I'll be right with you. I've got to summon all the people."

"Seriously? Summon who?" Debbie stood next to the light she wanted me to turn on. "Her grandmother is here."

"I know that, but I didn't know if I was supposed to tell her," I whispered and walked past Debbie on my way over to the light.

"Now you have to light the incense and use the feather to wave it around." Debbie pointed to the middle of the table, where she kept a candle along with the triangular-shaped incense she'd burn when I was here.

"Really?" I asked, keeping my voice down. "Why? She's here. Let's get this over with."

"No. I might be dead, and Jody might be my last client, but you have to give her a good reading. It has to be done right. My reputation depends on it, and David will have to live with what others have said about me." Debbie wasn't budging. "Light the candle. Light the incense."

I jerked the chain of the lamp and lit up the room. There were so many ghosts walking around. None of them appeared to see the others. They walked through each other and just wandered around.

"Don't mind them. They are just waiting for their loved ones to find me." Debbie shrugged. "I guess they'll leave once I don't come back."

I grabbed the long lighter off the table and did exactly what she'd told me to do, even though I wasn't doing it with pride like she wanted me to.

My hand shook when I lit the incense.

"What's wrong?" Debbie asked.

"I'm nervous. I don't like pretending to be you or even pretending to tell Jody anything from her grandmother." I picked up the small plate the incense was sitting on with one hand and the feather in the other. "I have no idea what I'm doing."

"I'll tell you everything you need to do for a reading. Step by step." Debbie didn't make me any less nervous. "Hold up the incense plate and swipe the smoke with the feather. Do it around the door and in all the corners." She showed me how to do it. "This will clear out the other spirits from this room, giving the grandmother her own space to be seen and heard. It filters the noise."

It was like Debbie had trained the wandering souls. Before I finished the first corner, the souls had disappeared, leaving the grandmother standing alone in the doorway.

"You will ask Jody to come in and have a seat, just like I do you." Debbie was so good at making me feel comfortable when I came to see her. I wasn't sure if I was going to be able to translate the same to Jody, but I'd try.

"After this, you've got some questions to answer." I had to use every opportunity I could to make sure she didn't disappear like my other Betweener clients loved to do. When the questioning began, it was like they didn't want to answer them.

It was the darnedest thing. They came to me for help, but when it was time for them to help me, they ghosted.

"Jody, you can come on in here," I called toward the door where I'd left her.

"You have to sit down like I do." Debbie pointed to her chair.

"Can't I just stand?" Goosebumps crawled up my spine at the thought of sitting in her space. She was a psychic, and I was not. I was just a simple undertaker.

"I found this in the door when I got here and forgot I took it." Jody's arm was extended, and her fingers pinched a business card. "It looks like the Sleepy Hollow sheriff stopped by to see you. He wants you to call him."

I gulped and took the card, trying not to shake or give her an alarm that I wasn't Debbie, and he was here because Debbie was dead. I was sure he was looking for the next of kin, which would let him release a statement to the public once Vernon Baxter gave him the preliminary report of how Debbie was murdered.

"Thank you." I took the card and tucked it into my front pocket. "Please, have a seat."

I waited for her to walk to her side of the table and sit down before I sat down.

"Your grandmother is here." I smiled across the table and saw the relief in Jody's eyes. "I'm guessing you're here for the brooch?"

"Yes," she gasped and brought her hands up to her chest. "Please tell her I'm so sorry. I should've seen all the signs she'd given. The broken leg, the girlfriend, not to mention the little incident with the police."

"We aren't here to discuss that." The grandmother stood next to Jody. "We are going to discuss your future."

"Can't you just tell me where the brooch is?" I asked the grandmother. "I mean, with all that's going on and all." I pointed between me and Debbie's ghost, suggesting she'd better make use of the time we had today since it was the last time Jody would get guidance from Debbie.

"Is that old bat not telling you where it is?" Jody's attitude suddenly went really south. "My Nana told me she was a real first-class biddy."

"Ummm…" Frantically I looked at Debbie. "What's going on here?"

"Souls can be tricky if you don't proceed the right way. They love to hold grudges. Especially with the living they left behind and who want something from them." Debbie casually nodded Jody's way like she didn't want

Jody to notice. "You should've asked Jody about her grandmother. Bring up loving memories."

"Geesh." This wasn't as easy as I'd hoped it was going to be. "Listen, she's here, and she wants to connect with you, but you've got to be a nice granddaughter."

"I'm her great-granddaughter. She was a real you-know-what to my nana and my mother. She was a ball-breaker if you know what I mean." Jody wasn't helping her case any. "They gave me this stupid brooch. I sold it, and now I want it back. I know she knows where it ended up because I got her little messages from the beyond." She waved her hand in the air. "I want her to stop ruining my life by haunting me. All the three a.m. wake-up calls with the water and other electronics, real cute!" Jody talked with her chin up to the sky.

"She's standing next to you," I told Jody, making her jump the opposite way out of her seat.

"Tell her to stop haunting me. If she tells me where the brooch is, then I'll give it to Billy." Jody used her finger to cross her heart.

"She said that last time." Grandmother didn't look so convinced. "I've got a stipulation."

"She said you didn't do that last time, and it's on one condition." I wanted to hurry this thing along.

"Yeah, what is it?" Jody questioned, crossing her arms.

"She has to go visit Billy. Then she can come back, and I'll tell her how to get the brooch back from the person she sold it to." It seemed like a reasonable request, only I wasn't going to be here when Jody got back, but I didn't care, so I relayed the message.

"You've got to be kidding me?" Jody smacked the table.

"Emma Lee?" The voice from the doorway made the grandmother disappear.

"Oh my!" Jody screamed and held her chest like she was going to have a heart attack. "You scared the crap out of me, kid."

"David." My eyes popped open, and my mouth went dry. "You're home."

"David," Debbie's voice cracked, and she ghosted over to him.

"A little help here," I said like Debbie was going to save the sinking ship I'd found myself on.

"Emma Lee, where's my mom?" He walked through Debbie toward me. "Are you doing a reading or something?"

"Who is Emma Lee?" Jody asked, her eyes darted between me and David.

"Jody, go see your brother. Granny said." I grabbed an unlighted incense and smacked it in the palm of her hand as I guided her toward the door. "Take this and put it in your house. Light it when you need to vent to your grandmother."

"Emma Lee, where is my mom?" David asked when I shoved past him.

"Who is Emma Lee, Debbie?" Jody jerked away from me and glanced over her shoulder and over mine at David.

"That's not my mom." David started to laugh. "My mom is Debbie."

"Kids." I rolled my eyes and opened the door to literally push her out. Debbie was no help. She stood there in silence staring at David like she'd never seen him before.

"Who are you?" Jody asked and planted herself on the small front porch after I had to give her a little nudge forward.

"Look at my baby," Debbie whined. "I can't believe he's so…" she paused. "Grown. College man."

"I'll see you once you get back from your brother's. Bye-bye." I shut the door and planted my back up against it. "David," I sighed and pushed off the door. "I've got something to tell you."

"Why were you just trying to act like my mom?" he asked.

"Tell him Emma. Just be there for him. Promise me." Debbie continued to float between me and David.

There was a solid knock on the front door.

"Don't get hung up on that." I tried to move around his questioning and get straight to the point.

The pounding on the door got louder.

"Listen, lady." I jerked the door open to give Jody a good piece of my mind. "I don't have time to…"

"Emma Lee?" Trevor stood on the other side of the door. Jody stood behind him.

"Emma Lee? Who is this Emma Lee?" She demanded. "Debbie, what's going on?"

"Debbie?" David and Trevor said in unison.

"That's Debbie Dually. She told me my great-grandmother is forcing me to go see my brother before she tells me where the brooch is so I can go back and get it so she'll stop haunting me." Jody sounded like a full bucket of crazy. "I gave her the sheriff card that was stuck in the door. Did you stick it in the door?"

"Is your great-grandmother in there?" Trevor asked her and tried to glance inside of Debbie's front door.

"She's dead. Debbie had called her from wherever it is their souls go." Jody pointed to me.

"Heaven." I nodded. "They go to heaven."

"Let me get this straight." Trevor leaned to one hip and rested his hand on the butt of his gun, which was stuck down into the holster around his waist. "Emma Lee told you your great-grandmother—"

"Debbie told me," Jody interrupted and folded her arms and shifted her tiny body to one side. "Right, Debbie?"

"Emma Lee Raines, you are under arrest for impersonation of a deceased person." Trevor ripped the cuffs right off his belt and reached to grab my wrist.

"Deceased?" David moved in front of me, not letting Trevor cuff me just yet. "My mom is Debbie Dually, and this is her client Emma Lee."

"David," I turned him to face me. "I came here to let you know that your mom has died."

"I came here to tell you that your mother has been *murdered*." Trevor could've been a little more sympathetic. David blinked a few times as if he were trying to process what was happening. "Emma Lee Raines was the last person seen with your mother, and they were arguing. Your mother was found deceased in the town square in Sleepy Hollow. On my way up here, the coroner called and informed me your mother had a large amount of cyanide in her system. She'd been poisoned."

"Emma? Did you?" David started to ask me, but I stopped him really fast.

"No. No, I didn't, and I think she knew someone was going to because she…" I stopped when I realized I was going to sound crazy if I told them how Debbie had insisted I tell her I could see dead people. "She said she was in fear of her life."

"Is that right?" Trevor asked and took another step closer.

David stepped aside like he was going to let Trevor take me.

"I'm so confused." David ran his hand over his head. "Mom called and asked me to come home early. I took my finals, and now she's gone."

"Emma, we have some business to take care of since you didn't come to the station to give a statement like I'd asked you, then I'll just go on and haul you down now for impersonation." Trevor gave no room for argument.

He slapped the cuffs on me, and on our way to his sheriff's car, he read me my rights.

"David, please drive the hearse back to Sleepy Hollow. Follow us," I yelled just as Trevor put his hand on top of my head and put in the car. "I'll tell you everything!" I gave one last plea before Trevor slammed the door.

I stared out the window at David, completely ignoring Jody. Debbie was next to him and trying to comfort him the best way a ghost mother could. He was sobbing. When Jody stepped over to touch him, Debbie glared at her.

I flipped my body around to watch David from the back window of the sheriff's car in hopes he'd jump in the hearse and follow me like I'd asked. He simply stood there and watched.

This had not turned out like I'd rehearsed in my head on the road trip to Lexington.

Not a bit.

Chapter Six

"I'm going to ask you one more time." The lines around Trevor's mouth deepened as the look of dissatisfaction about my one-word answers for the past two hours of his interrogating me had worn on him. "What were you doing impersonating Debbie Dually?"

"We were friends." I decided to give him a little more of an answer than a shrug. "I wanted to tell David about his mother before you did."

"You impersonated her. That doesn't look good. Do you understand, Emma Lee?" He didn't understand how him treating me like a three-year-old wasn't going to get him far. "I've got Debbie's client list, and we are interviewing every one of them. How many times have you pretended to be Debbie Dually? Are you sick? I mean, if you're… well… you know." He alluded to the fact my Funeral Trauma was back, and I didn't appreciate that at all.

"When is my lawyer going to get here?" I asked him through my gritted teeth.

After about a half hour of the initial interrogation and my lips staying shut, I could see this wasn't going well, so I'd lawyered up by calling Granny to get me an attorney, since I couldn't wait all day on a public defender.

"You didn't find any cyanide in my funeral home. You can't keep me," I told him after I made my phone call and Granny told me to tell him he had to charge me to keep me.

Technically, he could keep me for twenty-four hours, but I was going to use any tactic to get out of here.

"The public defender will get here when they can." Trevor was standing on the opposite side of the table, leaning on his fisted hands. "In the meantime, why don't you answer my question about what subject matter you and Ms. Dually were arguing over earlier this afternoon?"

"Trevor, you do know that you could stand to get a haircut. It just doesn't look good for the sheriff to be running around with longer-than-normal cop hair." It was time to buy more time.

There was no way I was going to tell him about why Debbie had come to see me.

"Emma Lee, I've about had it up to here with you." He had gone a little higher on the neckline than he'd done an hour ago when he'd said the same exact thing.

"When you get up to here"—I put my hand way above my head—"you let me know."

My eyes shifted to the sound of jingling bells right before a stream of white fog entered the far back corner of the room. I knew that jingle. It was Debbie's ankle bracelet.

Ghosts were a funny thing. They all came to me in different forms. Some I could touch. Most I could not. They were always dressed in the clothes they were killed in. Luckily for Debbie, she had on regular clothes. And the bells were a nice touch.

It helped signal her arrival before her appearance. That was important because it helped me prepare to see her and not get taken by surprise when she showed up like most of the other Betweener clients.

"My, my, my. Trevor O'Neil." Debbie tapped her temple. "Let me see."

Since Debbie had her incense and feather on her when she died, she had it in the afterlife too. I could only imagine all the clients she'd have in the great beyond.

"Tell him to remember where he came from and mind his manners or Nana would be awful disappointed in him." Debbie circled around using the feather to create the awfullest sight of smoke you ever did see. "She didn't raise him that way. And it wasn't why he'd become a cop. He needs to look at all the evidence."

If only Trevor wasn't there so I could ask Debbie what that evidence was and see if I could get to the real killer.

"Now, Trevor." I let out a long, deep sigh and placed my elbows on the table, leaning my chin on my hands like a little cup. "Do you think Nana would approve of your behavior? It seems you've had it out for me since the day you got here, and she didn't raise you like that."

He jerked up to standing. His face turned to stone.

"How do you know about her?" The tone of his voice shifted, almost eerie. "Have you been looking into my past?"

"I'm just saying that I know southern gentlemen, and you've not been very neighborly since you got here."

I was interrupted by the knock on the door.

We both turned to look at the small vertical window at the little man standing with his face planted up to the glass. He held up a badge.

"You're lucky your counsel is here, but we will revisit this later," Trevor warned and walked over to the door to let in what appeared to be my lawyer.

"Ernest Peabody." He was a short man, maybe five foot three at the most, with a bald spot on the back of his head and a comb-over so thin he should just do the right thing and go all bald. He had on a light-blue leisure suit and the brightest-white wing-tipped shoes I'd ever seen.

If this was the man that was going to try to get me out of here, then I might as well make myself comfortable. I shifted in the chair. It groaned, imitating how my insides felt.

He gave Trevor a card. "I'll be representing Ms. Raines, and you cannot hold her on fraud charges or impersonation. This is a joke. You know it, and I know it. I talked to the young lady outside who had gotten a psychic reading from Ms. Raines, and she did say that she was the one who cornered Ms. Raines at the home of Debbie Dually. She did in fact say that she'd go on record that Ms. Raines was apprehensive about Jody's insistences to have a reading since she was late to an appointment with Debbie Dually." Mr. Peabody rambled on and on, making my already swimming head a flood. "According to David Dually, Debbie's son, Emma Lee and his mother were good friends, and it wasn't unusual for Emma Lee to be in their home."

"Good boy." Debbie smiled with pride. "David." She smiled when she said his name. "He's got the gift, and I tried to contact him. I told him to help you."

That was good information to know that I'd wished I'd known before now. It was a gift I didn't have, but Debbie seemed to be wanting to work through me, and if I was going to get out of this mess, I was going to have to listen. It was how the Betweener client thing worked. I was at their mercy.

When Trevor tried to say something, Mr. Peabody spoke up again.

"Both Jody and David will give sworn statements saying the exact same thing." Mr. Peabody took a piece of paper from his briefcase and stuck it in Trevor's face. "So, unless you're going to charge my client with something that'll stick, I'm going to take her out of here."

"You do know about the evidence against Ms. Raines and the murder of Debbie Dually?" Trevor wasn't about to give up that easy.

"You mean how she and my client had met up at the funeral home earlier today, where you walked in on them, only overhearing part of a conversation?" Peabody laughed, scoffing at Trevor.

Trevor's face turned red.

"The victim was found at the scene with a glass mason jar, the exact kind of mason jar Ms. Raines leaves out for her clients to enjoy tea. And it just so happens, I saw the victim break one of those glasses with my own eyes." Trevor really thought he had this one in the bag. His confidence exuded from him.

I hated how he called Debbie a victim and not by her name. But Debbie didn't seem to mind. She stood next to Peabody and fanned him with the feather, probably putting some sort of thoughts in his head.

"You mean to tell me that Emma Lee Raines is the only person in the south from here to Lexington that drinks tea from a mason jar?" About that time, Mr. Peabody retrieved a mason jar from his briefcase. "Because I drink from them all the time. Plus, didn't you just tell me the one you saw Debbie Dually drinking from had broken?"

Trevor stood there in utter silence.

"Why don't you just move out of the way so me and Emma Lee can get out of here." Mr. Peabody waved me to get up.

"Hurry up, Emma," Debbie said before she ghosted, taking the plume of smoke with her.

I didn't waste a moment's time getting up and hurrying out the door with Mr. Peabody on my heels.

"Emma Lee!" Granny screamed from across the room and scampered out of her chair. Her eyes lit up when she saw me.

It wasn't when I saw Granny that I lost it. It was Jack Henry Ross in the chair next to her that made the tears free flow down my cheeks.

"Emma." I could feel the heat from his voice that made chills crawl along my spine after he'd embraced me, and the warmth of his protection wrapped around me like a blanket. "We need to get you out of here. Don't say another word."

"Ernest, you are a lifesaver." Granny took Ernest's hands in both of hers and looked him dead in the eyes. "I don't know how I'm ever going to repay you."

"Finally going out for that $2.99 blue-hair-special-plate supper down at the diner." He winked at Granny.

Though this was no time for flirting, Granny had always been the cat's meow among single elderly men, and she knew how to work a room like nobody's business.

"You old dog, you." Playfully, she smacked him on the light-blue suit coat and batted her eyes. "You make sure they don't charge my Emma with anything that has to do with that crazy psychic, and I'll see what I can do about that supper."

"Where can we talk?" Ernest had turned back to business.

"My office?" I suggested since it was the only place where I could control who had wandering eyes and nosy ears. "It's our safest bet."

All eyes were on us.

"Where is David?" I asked when I didn't see him.

"He drove the hearse here behind Trevor like you asked him to do, and Mazie gave him a ride back." Jack Henry knew Mazie had the inside scoop on my Betweener gig. "Let's not worry about that right now. We've got to focus on you. Things don't look good."

His words chilled me to the bone.

Chapter Seven

While Granny, Jack Henry, and Ernest Peabody sat in my office in Eternal Slumber trying to come up with different ways to get me off the suspect list for Debbie Dually's murder, I slipped down to the morgue in the basement to see if I could talk to Vernon Baxter.

There was a visible temperature change from the main level of the funeral home to the basement where the county morgue was located. Sleepy Hollow was a small community in the holler and between caves where tourists loved to flock to explore. When we needed a real morgue so we could avoid transporting bodies to Lexington every time there was a death, Vernon Baxter had received a grant from the state along with money from the city. He had gotten every piece of equipment imaginable, and all of it was the latest and greatest. I was banking on the real forensic evidence to be on my side.

The doors of the elevator opened. The cold whipped around me, making goosebumps along my arm. Vigorously I rubbed them to chase them away.

I pushed through the double metal doors that kept the really cold air inside of the actual morgue. Debbie Dually's body was lying on one of the exam tables, and Purdy Ford was on the other, with Mary Anna Hardy hovering over her head with a can of Aqua Net hair spray.

Mary Anna looked up at me and batted her blue eyes. She rushed over in her hot-pink high heels and hugged me to her chest. I couldn't help but look down at her big boobs toppling out of her white V-neck. Her short bleached-blond hair was styled exactly like Mary Anna's icon, Marilyn Monroe.

"Oh, honey." She chomped on gum like a cow chewing its cud. "Everything is going to turn out all right."

I already knew she was talking about me being a suspect in Debbie's death. Word got around like wildfire in Sleepy Hollow. Granted, more than half of it was gossip, and the more it was told, the saucier the tale got.

"I'll be fine," I assured her and stepped back. "The sheriff will find the killer."

"I can't believe it." Debbie Dually was sitting on the steel table next to her human body. Smoky incense spewed from her body. The bells around her ankles jingled as she swung her legs. "You know, Emma Lee, there's a lot of people who could've done this to me."

I gave her a sympathetic look.

Mary Anna went back over and picked up a comb and the can of Aqua Net to finish off Purdy Ford, an Eternal Slumber client whose funeral was in a couple of hours.

"Do you think you should be down here? Seeing as you're the number-one suspect." Vernon Baxter was a stately older man I was sure was the cat's meow in his younger years. His salt-and-pepper—more salt than pepper—hair along with his steel-blue eyes made him look very old-Hollywood debonair.

"Hush your mouth, Vernon." Mary Anna tsked. "You know our Emma Lee didn't hurt a flea, and someone is out to get her." She waved the comb around while she talked. "Do you think it's Burns Funeral? Bea Allen is so jealous of you right now with all your business. They ain't got nothin' going on over there." She rolled her eyes, took a step back, and took another go at Purdy Ford's bouffant hairdo with the comb. "She had the nerve to try to do one of their clients' makeup. The corpse looked like they'd straight up just left the carnival. The family called me, and hand to God"—she stuck one hand on her big boobs and the other with the comb in the air—"I had to work on the skin for two hours. Two hours. They paid me double, but still. Bea Allen knows better than to try to save a dime. But if you do go to trial, please let me do your hair. Jurors look at that kind of stuff, you know."

Mary Anna picked up the can of hair spray and gave Purdy's head a good soaking.

"I'm sure there's gonna be humidity up there with everyone gabbing about you and what happened." She pushed the spray nozzle a few more times. "Ain't gonna hurt to use more." She winked a big blue eye at me and chomped on the piece of gum in her mouth.

"That's exactly why I'm down here." I shook my head and walked over to my friend. "You both know I didn't do this, and I really need some evidence to prove it."

"From what I heard, you and Debbie here were having an argument before the Clarks found her." He gave me the idea that I had to go see the Clarks and find out what they knew.

"The Clarks found her?" I made that mental note.

"See, I've done said too much." He looked up from Debbie's body, his eyes magnified under the binocular-looking headset he had on.

"Cissie Clark has an appointment with me in about an hour. She and Purdy were in Jesus group together, and she's heading up the repast." Mary Anna mentioned the get-together after the funeral. "That's why I've got to get this head of hair done." She looked down at Purdy and groaned. "No wonder she had the perfect beehive all her life. I've never seen someone with so much hair."

"Maybe the beehive will die with Purdy." Vernon looked over at us and laughed.

"Vernon," I gasped. "That's awful."

"That hair sure is awful," he said, and we all laughed. Even Debbie laughed. It was the first time I'd seen her smile since… well… you know.

"Gosh. I needed that." I put my hand on my stomach. "I really could use y'all's help. Mary Anna, if Cissie just so happens to mention anything, do you think you could work your magic?"

"Honey, that woman's flips flap more than a leaky heart valve. I'm sure she'll be spilling her guts to anyone who will listen." Mary Anna grabbed her makeup bag. She took out a big brush that looked like a feather duster and swiped Purdy's face one more time. "She's already to go."

"Thank you. Good job. Better than when she was living." Vernon shrugged, making another snide remark.

"I'll let you know if I hear anything." Mary Anna packed up her cosmetics along with her hair products in her rolling bag and tugged it along behind her when she walked to the door. "Toodles."

"I'll have her dressed in about a half hour so you can get her up to the viewing room." Vernon and I both looked over at the casket that her family had picked out and was waiting for her.

Vernon would dress her and place her earthly body in its final bed. They'd picked out a nice oak with a cream interior. We might've made fun of Purdy's style of hair, but she was a good woman and always kind. She'd be sorely missed.

While he signed off on the paperwork for me to pay Mary Anna, I walked back over to Debbie and her ghost. She, too, would be missed by me.

"You didn't see anyone?" I asked her when Vernon had walked into his office to make a copy of Purdy's last spa treatment so I could put it in her file upstairs in my office.

"No one." She shook her head. "I did linger in the front viewing room of the funeral home while the Clarks came in to talk to you. There was a noise from the vestibule, but I figured it was one of your employees. When I walked out there, I thought it must've been Hettie coming back with more tea because there was a fresh glass of tea sitting there for someone to take." She looked down at herself. "I took it and walked outside to let the warm sunshine cover my face because I was mad at you for not confirming your gift. I was going to wait in the park for your clients to leave before I came back in to talk to you and apologize for how I behaved in your office."

"Forget about that. We need to figure out who did this." I reached out to see if I could touch her, but my hand went through her wispy body. "I'm going to need you to help me. You said there were a lot of people who might've wanted to kill you." I recalled her saying that earlier. "Can you give me some names?"

"There's a big psychic fair at the convention center in Lexington. You need to go there. I feel it." She put her hands out, the incense in one, the feather in the other. Her chin was lifted to the ceiling, and her eyes were closed. "David. You have to talk to David."

"I don't know. He doesn't want to see me right now." I shook my head. "Maybe I'll give him a day."

Not that I had a day. It was already six p.m. and there was no way I would make it to Lexington in time to get into the fair. I remembered the commercials on TV for it. The times were seven a.m. to seven p.m.

Trevor wouldn't be able to gather enough information to have me arrested by morning. I could get up early and get out of Sleepy Hollow before Trevor opened those green eyes of his.

"I don't think you done it either, but there's cyanide in her system that I was able to trace back to the drink in her glass." Vernon walked out of his office and picked right up from our conversation from earlier. "It's the same type of glass you have here. Did you count how many glasses you have up there? Is one missing? Are they all accounted for?"

"Vernon!" I bounced on my toes. "You're a genius. I still have the box they came in upstairs, and I can count them. I know there were twelve. But the cyanide. Where on earth did that come from?"

"That I do not know." His expression stilled. A much different look from when we were talking about Purdy.

Which reminded me that I needed to make sure all the arrangements upstairs were ready for her evening layout, followed up by her funeral. It was going to be a long walk to the cemetery.

"Let me know if you get any more clues from her body." I knew Vernon would go over Debbie's body twice for any sort of evidence that would lead us to the killer.

"There's always a silent piece of evidence the killer never realizes they left behind on a victim," Vernon's tone created a chill between us that seemed to grow, making us both shiver.

"Thanks, Vernon." I offered a peaceful smile that I wished would land in my knotted stomach. "Trevor can't arrest me on having tea served in a mason jar alone."

After we said our goodbyes and confirmed Purdy Ford would be ready in a half hour, I headed back upstairs to join the defense team.

"There you are. Where you been?" Granny's panties were in a wad when I walked back into my office.

"I had to go check on Purdy Ford and see when Vernon was going to be bringing her up." I grabbed Purdy Ford's file off my desk and flipped it open. I put Mary

Anna's time sheet and the paper Vernon had signed off on in the file.

Granny gave me the stink eye, and so did Jack Henry—both for different reasons. Granny was always looking to see if I had gotten the Funeral Trauma symptoms back, and Jack Henry was trying to figure out if my new Betweener client was there.

"Ernest, you got her?" Granny asked my new lawyer. "I've got to get back to the Inn so I can get my repast food on over to Cissie Clark's house. I want to make sure I'm leaving her in good hands."

"I'm not good hands?" Jack Henry gave Granny a goodbye hug.

"What house? I thought they were going to have it here?" I thumbed through the pages until I found the repast sheet where her family had specifically asked to use the viewing room next to Purdy's.

"Nope. Changed her mind a couple hours ago. Said it was best to have it at the house." Granny pinched her lips together as a big sigh escaped through her nose.

"She didn't call to tell me about the plans changing." I knew exactly what was going on here.

"Word has gotten around." Granny's words flew all over me.

Cissie Clark's little message was sent loud and clear without coming out and saying she wanted nothing to do with me or Eternal Slumber.

"Fine. If the Fords want to play that way and listen to Cissie Clark, I'll play that way," I warned and snatched up the folder.

"Emma Lee, now is not the time to be making any more enemies than you need to." Ernest peeled off the blue leisure jacket and hung it on the back of one of the chairs in front of my desk. He unbuttoned each cuff on his pale-pink shirt and rolled each sleeve up like we were about to get down and dirty.

"He needs to let go a little and relax." Debbie jingled her ghost self into the room. "If he's going to be asking all sorts of questions about my death, I should be here."

The new shadow of a ghost scooted in from the bathroom and stopped next to Debbie. The two of them seemed to have a conversation that I couldn't hear.

"Emma?" Ernest smacked his hands together. I didn't even see him sit down in the chair, much less scoot it up so he could have a surface to write on. "I have to know."

"Know what?" I took my eyes off the two ghosts.

"Can I see you for a second?" Jack Henry opened the door to my office. "Excuse us, Ernest."

"He sounds serious. I'm guessing he wants to know if you see me." Debbie ghosted through the open door.

"I'm sorry," I said to Ernest on my way out the door. "I'll be right back."

It was my ingrained southern roots that forced me to apologize. It was a way of life and taught to us at an early age.

Debbie and Jack were waiting for me in the vestibule. I took a quick look in Purdy Ford's viewing room. Vernon hadn't brought her up yet. I looked at my watch, and the funeral was going to be starting in an hour. There were things that needed to be done. It was a job, and no matter if I was a suspect, life still went on.

"Where are you going?" Jack Henry didn't sound very pleased with me. "This is serious, Emma, and I don't like how you're just ignoring it. I know you see Debbie. I can tell by the way you're acting, and if she doesn't get the fact that it doesn't look good for you, then you've got to find a way to get out of this. Trevor O'Neil isn't going to stop.

He's already mad about the parking tickets, so I paid them for you."

"I have to get Purdy's funeral ready." I was happy to see that John Howard Lloyd had already put all the chair covers on the viewing chairs. I walked down the rows and ran my hand over all of the fabrics on the tops of the chairs to take out any wrinkles. "Yes. I see her. She's also got a lot of ghosts following her."

John Howard had also left the memorial cards on the first seat in the front of the viewing room. I picked them. I smoothed out the long window curtains on my way back to put the cards on the stand where the mourners could sign the family's register and pick one of the cards up.

"Debbie." Jack Henry was so cute in how he talked to the Betweener clients even though he couldn't see them. "It's so important to tell Emma who might have something against you."

"There's Goddess Jillian, who loves to try to go by 'Debbie' and imitate me." Debbie held up her hand and started to count off the people. "Mystic Mervin, Warrioress Roma, and Angela Ariel, to name a couple that are in town for the psychic convention."

I hurried back to the stand, where I put the cards down, grabbed the pen out of the holder, and quickly wrote down the four names she gave me.

"This is a great start." I looked at Jack. "Goddess Jillian, Mystic Mervin, Warrioress Roma, and Angela Ariel."

Debbie could hear Jack Henry and everyone else, making it nice for me to not have to repeat everything back to my Betweener clients.

"Any last names?" He looked over my shoulder.

"When we take our oath as a provider to the spirit world, we don't keep a last name professionally. I have mine because of David." Debbie's shoulders slumped. "Oh, David," she cried out.

"I'll go see David. I promise. Let's do what Jack Henry said and get some sort of leads to check out before Trevor locks me up and I can't do anything to help you." The importance of finding out who would be upset with Debbie was starting to settle in.

"I'll go get on my database and look up these people." Jack Henry didn't seem so positive when he took the card and looked over the names again. "Maybe a couple of them have some sort of record. That'd be great if they did." Jack

Henry gave me a quick kiss. "I'll be back for the funeral procession."

"I love you," I told him.

"I love you, and this is why we need to get this all cleared up." He reached out and squeezed my hand before taking off.

"Are they at the convention?" I asked Debbie and straightened the cards on the stand next to the signing book.

"They are making appearances on different panels, but they aren't from our area. They come from all over the world," she noted.

"How long is the convention?" I asked, knowing it was of the utmost importance to get there before it was over. I flipped open the signing book to the middle and ran my finger down the center to crack the spine so it lay flat on the stand. Satisfied, I flipped it back to the first page and was happy to see my little trick worked.

"Only four days. Today is the first day, so the quicker the better." The other ghost appeared next to her. "Emma, this is Ernest's wife. He's been talking to her every night since she passed, and she wants him to know that she loves him, but he needs to ask Zula out." She did a little skedaddle with her fingers, shooing me away. "Go on and tell him so Kate can rest in peace."

"You want me to go in there and tell him that I see his dead wife and she wants him to date my granny?" I laughed.

"Who wants to date Zula Fae?"

The voice caused me to jerk around.

My elbow caught the stand. I reached out to stop it from teetering, but I wasn't quick enough. It tumbled to the ground, scattering the cards all over the place.

"Who are you talking to, Emma Lee?" Bea Allen Burns had snuck into Eternal Slumber without me hearing her. She was looking at all the cards on the floor. Her heavy lashes that shadowed her cheeks flew up to meet my eyes. "Are you sick?" Her face looked like she was weaned on a pickle.

Chapter Eight

"Are you sick? She asked if you were sick?" Mazie asked about Bea Allen when I told her about the little visit.

We stood in the back of the viewing room while Purdy Ford's loved ones went by the casket to get one last view of her and a last goodbye before Pastor Brown did his sermon to send her off.

"Can you believe her?" I'd found myself opening up more and more to Mazie about my personal life, not just my Betweener life.

It'd been a long time since I'd had a really good friend. In high school I wasn't so popular. Let's face it, living in a funeral home wasn't the coolest thing for a teenager, and certainly no teenage boy considered it a good thing to date the funeral home girl. That was the nickname the mean girls in high school gave me, and it stuck.

"She's so nosy." Mazie didn't say anything I didn't already know.

The funeral was going fine. I didn't even bother saying anything to Purdy's family about the repast. I took Granny at her word, and she was right. I'd already had one falling-

out with Bea Allen when she first showed back up in
Sleepy Hollow after being gone for years. I was smart
enough to know not to chew my cabbage twice.

"Did David say anything?" It was a good opportunity
to ask her about the drive back.

"I did get some information about some clients to look
into." Mazie dug in her purse and pulled out a piece of
paper. "This guy had come to the house several times
before David left for college. He claimed that Debbie had
told his wife he was cheating. He was there to confront her.
Plus he dragged his wife with him a few times. Debbie
never answered the door." She pulled out another sheet of
paper and unfolded it. "David said his mom didn't want to
call the cops, but he did. There was a police report and
everything." She handed me a printed-out version of the
report. "I went back to the library and did a little research."

I scanned the paper and found the address of the man
and a statement from David, not Debbie.

"This is great." I looked at her with wide eyes and a
little excitement.

"That's not all. David said he had checked the caller
ID at Debbie's business before he drove your hearse to
Sleepy Hollow, and that guy had been calling consistently

since David had gone off the college." Mazie nodded. "This guy has been stalking her."

"How did you know that?" I asked about her allegations.

"David told me there were also daily messages from the guy."

"Did David let you listen to them?" I asked with urgency because those needed to be turned over.

"I asked to listen to them, but he wouldn't let me. He was odd. He said that he had to think things through and listen." Mazie rolled her eyes. "Whatever that means."

"Listen?" I wondered if he meant he was trying to hear from Debbie.

"I thought we'd head to this address tomorrow and check this guy out," Mazie suggested.

"There's a few places I have to go. The Psychic Convention is my first stop, then I'll see David." I shook the paper. "And now this."

"What time?" Mazie bounced with excitement. "Tomorrow is my off day."

"Six a.m." I told her the convention was open from seven a.m. to seven p.m. "The quicker I get out of Sleepy Hollow, the fewer chances Trevor has to stop by."

I looked up to the front of the viewing room, where the Auxiliary women had gathered around Purdy Ford. Beulah Paige waved Mazie up there.

"It's time to give our memorial. I'll be here by six a.m.," Mazie said over her shoulder on her way up the middle of the viewing room.

After all the women gave a fond memory of Purdy, Pastor Brown got up to the podium.

The sleeve on his brown pin-striped suit coat was a little too small, hitting above his wrist bone, exposing a tarnished metal watch. His razor-sharp blue eyes made his coal-black, greasy comb-over stand out.

"That man needs a new suit." Debbie Dually had ghosted up next to Purdy.

I laughed and tried not to, but Debbie was getting a good look at our local preacher.

"Emma Lee," Granny scoffed from the back row.

Bea Allen Burns was sitting in the row in front of Granny, and I couldn't help but notice she'd turned around.

Granny noticed, too, because she hopped up and grabbed me by the elbow, dragging me out of the viewing room.

"You better hide that crazy because I heard Bea Allen Burns is using your little murder rap against you. She landed the Clarks' arrangements today. You laughing at a funeral is a downright disgrace." She snapped her beady eyes at me. "Do you understand?"

"Yeah." I looked into the viewing room and noticed Bea Allen was still watching us.

"Remember." Granny was about to give me some of her sound advice. "You can't make a silk purse out of a sow's ear." She patted my arm. "I'm going to finish this funeral for you. Ernest said you didn't talk to him about the case."

"I will. I have to still run the business." Granny had sold the funeral home to me, which made her more than qualified to finish the service.

"No. You need to go on over to the Inn where Ernest is having supper and answer his questions." There was no wiggle room in Granny's request. She meant business, and no one ever went against what Zula Fae Raines Payne said, or they would meet a side of her you never wanted to cross.

I gave the viewing room a good once-over before I took Granny's advice and walked across the town square toward the Inn, stopping at the gazebo where Debbie was found by the Clarks.

"Come back to the scene of the crime?" Debbie appeared, as did Kate, Ernest's wife. "Or are you on your way to tell Ernest about Kate since you didn't do it earlier?"

"Debbie, you know I can't go around telling people their dead loved ones are sending them messages. They will tell Granny who will tell Doc Clyde," I hummed. "Maybe not Doc Clyde since they are on the outs. But whichever doctor she tells will have me locked up."

"How on earth do you think Zula Fae is going to find everlasting love if Ernest isn't going to let go of Kate?" Debbie asked, playing matchmaker.

"I guess Ernest will have to come to an agreement with himself." I sucked in a deep breath.

"But how is Kate supposed to go on and live her afterlife?" Debbie swept alongside of me and Kate did too.

"When I find out who killed you, and you go to the great beyond, you can take care of Kate." It was a logical explanation since Kate wasn't a Betweener client, which made me not responsible for telling Ernest anything.

I stomped up the steps of the Inn without Debbie following me. Ghosting away after I refused to do something the client wanted me to was one of the characteristics each Betweener client had in common. It was like they were punishing me, and in Debbie's case, she very well might be because it was my life that was really on the line.

There was nothing better than the smell of fried corn bread and brown-bean soup. Especially when Granny made it. The smell of Crisco and onions swirled around me before I even opened the screen door and walked into the Inn.

Crisco was one of the secret ingredients Granny put in her bean soup. It was definitely not low in calories. Neither was the fried corn bread. The sound of silverware and murmuring floated from the dining room.

"Gross." Debbie reappeared, alone this time, pinching her nose. "I can't stand onions." Her voice contorted from cutting off her nasal passages.

It was hard to protest Debbie's dislike for onions as I ignored her and walked into the dining room to find Ernest Peabody.

"Where is that awful blue jacket?" Debbie drifted above the room.

I stood up on my tiptoes to get a look over the tops of the heads.

Dusk filled the mountains with purple mist and streamed through the dining room through the back wall that was all glass. The Inn had a picturesque view like no other place in Sleepy Hollow. All the tables were filled, and most of the patrons were eating bean soup and corn bread. A few of Granny's waitstaff were busying themselves with refilling tea and water glasses.

"I don't see him," Debbie reported back to me.

Me either, I thought to myself, making sure I didn't respond to Debbie.

I took a quick look in the gathering room across the hall and found Ernest in a huge stack of cream pillows sitting on the large brown couch. The blue leisure suit matched Granny's baby-blue floor-to-ceiling drapes perfectly.

"Mr. Peabody," I greeted him with a smile. He sat up. "Granny is going to finish up Purdy Ford's funeral for me so I could come talk to you. I'm sorry about earlier."

"Fine." He gave a hard nod and picked up his briefcase off the floor. He put it on the coffee table with a thud.

"Before you start, I do have some information about some of the people in Debbie's industry that might have a motive." I hadn't figured out what the motive was, but it was the list of names Debbie had given me. I took Purdy's memorial card, which I'd written the names on, out of my crossbody bag and handed it to him. "You can write those names down if you want. I'd like to have the paper back."

"Who are these people?" Ernest asked after he'd scanned the list.

"They are psychics that've had some type of issue with Debbie Dually in the past. I never had an issue with her. She was my advisor." I tried to be as vague as I could be.

"Advisor? You believe in all the mumbo googly jumbo?" There was a hint of laughter in his voice that seemed to mock me.

"I try not to make fun of anyone's beliefs." I didn't even tell him I believed in God, or he would have given me all sorts of reasons believing in a psychic was wrong. The same song and dance Doc Clyde had given me when I tried to explain to him that I did see spirits.

I'd embraced the reasoning that I'd become a Betweener as a gift from God, to be able to help people cross over while bringing justice to their demise. It was my way of accepting that I saw them. My purpose in life. Once I'd realized my gift, my stress level had gone way down, but my life had gotten a lot more complicated.

"Did she tell you something in your future you didn't like and that's what your argument was about?" he asked, clearly trying to give motive for being a suspect.

"No. She'd given me a reading a few years back, and she came to see me to make sure I was doing what she saw as my future." It wasn't a lie. Debbie had asked me to confirm my duties as a Betweener. To see murdered spirits.

"Why was she yelling?" He took a file out of his briefcase and opened it. "According to sworn testimony from the Clarks and the sheriff, she was yelling at you about between something. What was between you that she wanted resolved?"

"Between something?" Debbie came into the room. "Betweener! Tell him I wanted you to make sure you could see me after I'd seen my own death."

"Own death," I gasped and threw my hand over my mouth. It was the first time Debbie had admitted she did see her own murder before she was killed.

"Death? Your death?" Ernest was all confused.

"I was saying that I'd rather see my own death than Debbie's. She was a wonderful woman, and I had no reason to kill her." I pointed to the memorial card. "I'm sure if you go to the psychic convention and talk to those people before they leave town, they might give you some insight into Debbie and her career."

"I'll write these down and see if my secretary will go check out the convention, but my number one priority is Zula… err… keeping you out of jail." Ernest let it slip that he was only helping me as a favor for Granny.

Debbie Dually's eyes grew big as she gave a couple of quick nods. Encouraging me to say something about Kate. Kate was next to her, with a look of compassion on her face.

"You know, Ernest," I sat down next to him and put my hand on his back. "Granny is awful smitten with you, and I think you should ask her out, regardless of what happens with me."

"She is?" Beads of sweat instantly formed along his brow line.

I reached over to the coffee table and plucked a tissue from the Kleenex box and handed it to him.

"I don't know, Emma Lee." He wiped the napkin all over his face. "Every time I go to ask her to go courting, I break out into a sweat. I've only ever done that one other time."

"With Kate?" I asked with a slight smile on my face.

"How did you know?" His jaw opened, and his brows furrowed. "There's no way you could've known I was a sweating mess for my entire married life."

"I know Kate and you were married for a long time, and it could only be Kate that you think about and may be holding you back from dating someone like Granny." The more I talked about him and Kate, Kate's ghost drifted farther and farther away from Debbie.

"Go on," Debbie Dually was rubbing her hands together. "Go in for the big kill."

"I think Kate would want you to have some companionship. That's all." I patted his back. "You don't have to date Granny or even marry her, just go to supper every once in a while or maybe watch a movie."

"He hates movies," Debbie blurted out. "He loves to bake."

"Maybe not a movie. Granny can't sit still for that long." I smiled, hoping it was a good cover. "You know, I'm not sure how you feel about cooking or baking."

"Baking?" He interrupted me. "Oh, I love baking."

I fanned my hands out in front of me.

"Perfect. Granny loves the kitchen, and she's always cooking and baking. I bet if you have some amazing recipe, she'd love to feature it in the diner." I nodded with raised brows.

"I do make some really good lemon squares." His face was lit up. "Kate loved them."

"Maybe you should keep the part about how Kate loved them to yourself." It was merely a suggestion because Granny would want Ernest all to herself and not have to share with his deceased wife.

"Good idea. Geez, Emma Lee." He grabbed his cell phone out of his briefcase. "I think I'll ask Zula right now."

"She's at the funeral, remember?" I reminded him. "She's there because I'm here to answer any questions you need to ask me about Debbie Dually."

There was a little ruckus in the corner of the room between Debbie and Kate. When I looked up, Kate was barely visible. She blew a kiss Ernest's way.

He lifted his face and set his eyes on the corner, though I was sure he couldn't see her. He lifted his hand to his cheek.

"I think Kate would approve of some companionship with Zula." Ernest grinned.

Chapter Nine

Debbie didn't stick around for the questioning after Kate had slipped away upon finding her peace in the afterlife. Then Ernest realized Granny just might be a catch, and he should ask her out.

In fact, he didn't even wait for me to leave the room when Granny had gotten back to the Inn from the funeral procession. He asked her if they could have a baking date, and she jumped at it.

That was my cue to hightail it out of there and get home. I had a big day ahead of me tomorrow and was ready to hit the sack.

Instead of crossing over the town square to walk back to the funeral home, I took the long way around and walked Main Street.

Doc Clyde's office was in the first building, followed by Higher Ground Café. There were small picket fences between the coffee shop and the courthouse. The courthouse was the tallest building in the Sleepy Hollow downtown area and right in the middle of Main Street.

Dong, dong, dong!

I practically jumped out of my skin when the courthouse clock dinged nine times, signaling it was nine p.m. I hurried past, knowing Sleepy Hollow would soon be in full darkness and ready for the night slumber. The crickets had started to rub their legs, the tree frogs were singing their songs, and the fireflies had already started to flutter about, making it appear as if twinkling lights were all over the mountainous background.

I hurried past the courthouse and noticed a sale on steaks in the window of Artie's Meat and Deli, which reminded me to see when Jack Henry was going to be off work so I could fix him a romantic supper. When I turned up the street to head toward Eternal Slumber, I noticed Girl's Best Friend Spa still had lights on.

My curiosity got to me, knowing that Mary Anna Hardy was going to snoop around to see what she'd heard about Debbie Dually's death and how everyone thought I was involved, so I decided to walk past the street the funeral home was on to go the spa.

Mary Anna was sweeping up hair when I looked through the window. When I tapped on it, she saw me and waved me in.

"Why are you here so late?" I asked.

"You know me. Purdy Ford's funeral was smack-dab in the middle of people's appointments after work. They didn't want to miss their weekly blowouts." She talked with her hands and chomped on her gum. "I told them to come on in after the funeral, and I'd get them in." She sighed. "Where you going this time of the night?"

The Girl's Best Friend Spa was the typical small-town hair salon.

"I was at the Inn and heading back home for some much-needed shut-eye," I said right before Fluggie Callahan emerged from the bathroom.

Her fanny pack was clipped around her waist. She wore a long-sleeved white tee that was tucked into her pants, which were about three inches too short and pulled plumb up to her armpits. She had on a pair of white tennis shoes and a camera around her neck. Her usual outfit.

"Well, well. Just the person I wanted to see." An evil grin crept up on her face. "I'm surprised you came in here with my car parked right outside."

I turned around and looked out the window at her beat-up wood-paneled station wagon parked in front of Girl's Best Friend Spa. I wanted to kick my own self in the butt because I wouldn't have come in if I'd seen it.

"What happened to your eyelashes?" I blurted out a question that wasn't filled with manners. Her white lashes were now black, making her look completely different.

"You like?" She came towards me with her eyes wide open for me to get a good look. She took her big glasses off her face and rotated her chin left, then right, then left again. "I had them dyed."

Mary Anna obviously didn't touch Fluggie's hair. Her sandy-blond hair was pulled up in the normal scrunchie-and-bobby-pins look she always seemed to be going for. I wondered why she didn't dye her lashes to match her hair.

"Let's not fuss about appearances. You know I'm not one to make a big deal out of how I look." She unzipped her fanny pack and took out her notebook. "Do you have a statement for the *Sleepy Hollow News* on the murder of Debbie Dually?"

"Fluggie Callahan, I'd be ashamed." Mary Anna was quick to come to my rescue. She said a few things, but Debbie Dually had ghosted in, and what she had to say caught my attention.

"A regular." Debbie sighed and floated around Fluggie. "Never really did what I told her was in her future."

I practically gasped when I heard Debbie say that Fluggie was a client.

"What did you want to know about her? You were a client of Debbie's, weren't you?" I gave Fluggie the back-off look when I'd noticed her stiffen.

"I went to see her once," Fluggie protested.

"Once a week," Debbie snorted. "Like a lot of regulars."

"Yes. You went to see Debbie Dually once a week." I snapped my fingers. "But you didn't do what she'd suggested." I grabbed Fluggie and gave her a huge hug. I let go and left her standing there speechless. "Thank you, Fluggie!" I yelled over my shoulder on my way back out the door. "Mary Anna, I'll talk to you tomorrow."

I practically ran down all the way back to Eternal Slumber, not alone.

"What on earth was that about?" Debbie swept in front of me and behind me.

"You said you had regulars. Fluggie didn't do what you suggested. Why? Did she not like what you had to say?" The answers to the questions didn't matter. What mattered were the clients' responses to what Debbie had told them. "Did you make them mad? Mad enough to murder you?"

"I…" Debbie appeared to have stumbled over her thoughts. "I guess some could be mad. I mean, I do have the one guy, though he's not a client, but his wife was."

"Yes. I heard about him through Mazie. David told her. That guy could be your killer. What did you say to his wife?" I asked and walked down the driveway on the far side of the funeral home where the entrance to my apartment was located.

After my sister Charlotte and I had taken over Eternal Slumber from Granny, Charlotte had a house to live in, but I didn't. We'd redecorated and did a little construction in the back of the first floor to create a small apartment. It was nothing fancy. A bedroom with a small kitchenette and a family room with just a couch and TV.

When I unlocked the door, I thought I was alone. I threw my keys on the small table right inside and heard the TV. The family room was on the left, and my bedroom was on the right.

"Where have you been?" Jack Henry had one arm over the back of the couch and had turned over it to look at me.

"I called Zula when you didn't answer my text, and she said you'd left a while ago."

"You aren't going to believe this, but Fluggie Callahan was a regular of Debbie's. Like once a week." I walked around the couch and sat next to him, letting him wrap me up in his big arms. "Not only that, but Debbie had a customer who she must've told something very important. The customer's husband has been stalking Debbie ever since. There's a record of the police being called." As I talked, I could see the look on Jack Henry's face start to change. There was some jaw clenching and eye twitching that told me what was coming, but I still continued to talk. "David said there are phone messages on Debbie's answering machine and everything. That's a motive if I've ever heard one. Plus, she's got regulars like Fluggie who don't take her advice. What if one of them killed her because they didn't like what she said?"

That must've been the straw that broke the camel's back for Jack Henry. He slowly uncurled his arms from around me and scooted a little away from me, getting a good straight-on look at me.

"Emma Lee, I know you need her to cross over, and all of these are great leads, but I can't let you go investigate all of this. It needs to be turned over to Trevor." Jack Henry had lost his marbles. "You need to stay far away from everything and everyone. I stopped by to see Trevor, and he told me he was keeping a close eye on you because Beulah Paige told him you liked to do your own snooping in other cases."

"That…" I had to bite my tongue not to curse her. "You know me. You know I'm not going to sit in this funeral home and work on Peter Shelton's funeral that's not for two days."

Poor guy. He'd been sitting on ice for three days already. He died of old age, but his family was scattered all over the states, and they were all coming, so that meant we couldn't get Peter's body in the ground until they all came in for the funeral.

"About that." Jack Henry scooted to the edge of the couch and clasped his hands in between his legs. "The Shelton family had him moved to Burns while Purdy's funeral procession was on to the cemetery."

"They what?" I jumped to my feet. "I was going to use that money to pay for Ernest Peabody's fees." I started to pace back and forth. "I bet this was all Bea Allen Burns's fault," I said through my gritted teeth.

"Calm down. We will get through this." Jack Henry didn't sound so sure, but those were the only hopeful words he had. "The Fenwicks and Pastor Brown also left notes saying they were going to change their preneed arrangements."

He didn't need to know, but I was going to go see Bea Allen at some point tomorrow. She was deliberately using this little murder rap to steal my business from me, and I was going to stop her, no matter the cost.

It was then and there that I knew I had to keep any and all information about Debbie's killer and my investigation from Jack Henry. He might not be the sheriff of Sleepy Hollow anymore, but he was still going to play by the book. That wasn't how I got the murders of my Betweener clients solved. It definitely wasn't how I was going to get Debbie's solved with me being the one under the magnifying glass.

Chapter Ten

The alarm went off way too early. Normally, I'd hit the snooze button a few times before I got out of bed, but not today! Being the number-one suspect in a murder investigation and really wanting to get out of town to gather more clues for your case were motivation to get up.

Plus, Mazie was already standing at my door with a cup of coffee in hand.

"Bea Allen is sabotaging Eternal Slumber," I groaned in the passenger seat of Mazie's car when we passed Burns Funeral on our way to Lexington.

I was happy to accept her offer to drive. It was hard to be in disguise when you drove a hearse. There was no way I wanted to attract any attention to myself at the psychic convention.

"She's gotten so ruthless since she moved back. They keep trying to get her to join the Auxiliary, and I keep voting her down." Mazie was good at driving with one hand and drinking her coffee with the other. "It's a unanimous and anonymous voting system."

"No wonder they never want to let me in." I took a drink of the coffee. "I'm sure it's Beulah who votes me out," I laughed. "Though I was close to getting in after my trial period."

"Really it's just a big gossip session." She didn't tell me anything I didn't already know because I'd been the brunt of their gossip circle many times. "What's our plan today?"

"I want to check out a list of psychics at the convention. Debbie gave me a few names, and she said they would be good ones that might not like her too much." I'd not seen Debbie since last night. "I don't have any solid facts about them. I wanted to ask Debbie about each of them, but when I got home last night, Jack Henry was there, and he's not wanting me to snoop since I'm a suspect."

"That's why you should snoop." Mazie and I had the same thoughts.

There was a lot more chitchat on our forty-five-minute drive to Lexington about different things. We changed from subject to subject. It was nice to finally have a friend I could just talk to.

"Where's the list?" Mazie drove around the parking lot of the convention center until she finally found a parking spot in the very last row.

I dug into my purse to pull out Purdy's memorial card.

"I think we should split up the names and find them on our own. And I'll run them through my library database." She ripped the memorial card in half, giving me Goddess Jillian and Mystic Mervin. She took Warrioress Roma and Angela Ariel. "These names," Mazie giggled and unhooked the seat belt.

"I can't get over how busy this place is already." I noted the time as exactly seven a.m., opening time. There was a line out the door and around the building as the crowd trickled in the entrance. "Oh!" I jumped with excitement. "I almost forgot to tell you how Debbie told me Fluggie Callahan was a regular client."

"Shut up!" Mazie smiled so big. "That's awesome. You can totally use this little bit of information against her."

"Against her?" I asked. My gut knotted at the sound of it.

"Yeah. She hurried into the library last night." Mazie rubbed her eyebrows. "Wait until you see what she did to her lashes."

"I did see." Fluggie must've gone straight to the library after I left Girl's Best Friend Spa. "What time did she stop by?" I asked.

"It was nine-something. I was putting away all the carts of books gathered throughout the day to get the library ready for this morning, and she said she needed to use the research computer." Mazie gave a sly grin and slanted a brow. "Of course I headed straight over to the computer when she left and checked out the history."

"Mazie, I love you," I gushed and squeezed her forearm.

"You think people would be smarter than that and erase any sort of searching they do on a public computer, but they don't." Mazie shook her head and got her money out as we got to the front of the line to buy our tickets at the ticket window.

"And?" I asked, holding up one finger so the attendant behind the window would charge me for one ticket.

"She looked up Debbie and traced back to Debbie's roots." She dug deep in her purse, nearly tripping over her feet when we pushed through the turnstile to enter the convention center. She pulled out some folded papers. "I printed them for you. Debbie Barnett was a transplant from New Orleans where she was born and raised. She married a guy with the last name of Dually, but they weren't married but three months. I'm not sure what happened, but there's a divorce decree in there that doesn't look like it was finalized. It's got all his information on there, but I didn't bother looking him up."

I stepped out of the way of the entrance to take a look at the papers Mazie had given me. Not finalized? This was a bit of interesting news that I'd be sure to ask Debbie once she appeared.

"I wonder if she still kept in touch with him? Or does David? Because I dug up a lot of his financials where he'd filed bankruptcy a few times since they were divorced." Mazie had really done some research, thanks to Fluggie's lead.

"Did Fluggie look all this up?" I asked.

"She only researched Debbie's background but nothing about her life here. I got to wondering about David and who his dad was, so that's when I decided to check into him. Interesting enough, he did get remarried to someone named Dee Holt." She gestured for me to flip the pages. "I have the wedding certificate in there along with a current address."

"You are amazing." There was a little bit of hope coursing through my veins that suddenly made me awake. "I'll check into them too."

My list of things to do and people to see was growing. How was I going to fit it all in and beat Trevor to the punch? From what Jack Henry had told me, Trevor seemed to be on top of it and had definitely done research. But, did he know how to do research like a librarian?

Doubtful.

Mazie and I had made plans to meet back in a couple of hours. It wasn't likely we would be finished quicker than that. By the looks of all the rows of psychics there, it was going to take two hours to even walk, much less talk to any of them.

Each psychic had a different setup. Some of them offered readings right there on the spot, while others were taking appointments for later in the day. They had taken this convention seriously. Fancy oriental rugs on the floor with stand-up folding screens to hide the private readings were pretty common in most of the booths.

There were some vendors who were selling witch balls, incense like Debbie Dually used in her readings, along with other things I'd never seen before, much less knew how to use. Nor did I want to find out.

"You." One of the psychics swirled a finger at me. "You have a gift. I can see them," she gestured behind me.

I turned around to look, and there was Debbie. She was floating behind me with her hands behind her back.

"But you aren't here to help people today." The psychic's eyes glowed with excitement. "You are here to find… mmmm… yes." Her seductive voice scared me. "Row thirty-four."

"She was always nice to chat with." Debbie had decided to finally join me.

"Thank you," I said to the psychic, wondering if she really knew I was looking for two different people on my list, which was in my pocket, so I wasn't sure how she knew.

"I can see the apprehension on your face. Remember, she's psychic." Debbie loved reminding how I still had a hard time wrapping my head around my gift, let alone trying to figure out anyone else's special talent. "They all know you're here to see someone."

It was then that I noticed all the psychics would come to the edges of their booths and look at me when I passed. There was a knowing look in their eyes, and it sent a chill through me.

I hurried as quick as my legs would take me to row thirty-four but not without abruptly stopping when I saw David Dually heading toward the exit door. Debbie's ghost darted after him and floated through the door after he left.

Why was he here? I wondered and made a note to be sure to ask him about it when I stopped by the house to see him. Another stop on my list.

Row thirty-four was different than the other rows of psychics. These were couples who were psychics. Just like the other psychics, the couples would emerge from their seats or from behind their screening to look at me. When I passed by one booth where no one greeted me, I stopped and looked at their sign.

"Goddess Jillian and Mystic Mervin are here to help you connect with your spirit animal." I read the exact two names on my list. "Are these them?" I turned to see if Debbie had caught back up to me.

No chance. She'd left me high and dry… again.

"Hello?" I called into the booth after I hadn't seen anyone.

"Welcome. I'm Goddess Jillian." A woman with a green scarf wrapped around her head and bracelets from her wrists to her elbows on both arms whipped around the wood screen. "Would you like a reading from me and Mystic Mervin?"

When I heard a familiar jingle, I looked down at her ankles. She was wearing the same ankle bracelet Debbie Dually wore.

"I like your anklet," I mentioned to break the ice.

"Mystic Mervin"—she projected his name—"got it for me."

A man, who apparently was Mystic Mervin, emerged from the back of the booth, wiping his mouth off.

"Sorry about that," he mumbled under a mouthful of food. "Reading auras and stuff gets you hungry."

"Auras?" I looked back up at their sign. "I thought you did spirit animals."

Goddess Jillian nudged him with a sly elbow, but it wasn't so inconspicuous.

"I mean, you're a fluttering goddess yourself." There was a certain charm to the middle-aged man.

"I've never been to a psychic convention," I said and tried to think fast at how I could get them to open up. "I'm not sure how all of this works."

"You can have your spirit animal come here or to our new location that we've just opened here in Lexington." Goddess Jillian looked younger than Mervin. She was eager to give me her card.

It was also different than the ones I'd seen at the other booths. Most of them had websites and the types of readings the psychics did, along with backgrounds that looked like something a psychic would have on their cards.

Goddess Jillian's was white with black ink and looked as if she'd cut it with a pair of dull scissors. Not professional.

"You moved here?" I asked.

"Mm-hmm." She ho-hummed and smiled. "Would you like to know your spirit animal?"

"You know, I did go to a local psychic a couple of times. In fact, I read in the paper today that she was murdered." I tapped my temple with the corner of her business card like I was trying to remember Debbie's name. "Darlene? Denise?" I questioned as I threw out bogus names. "Debbie! Her name was Debbie. So sad. I guess you could say I'm looking for a new spiritual leader."

"Excuse us," Mystic Mervin interrupted us and jerked Goddess Jillian behind the screening. It was obvious saying Debbie's name got his full attention.

While they continued to talk in hushed whispers, I couldn't help but notice some open luggage off to the side with several stacks of their business cards inside. The dangling leather luggage tag with something written on it caught my attention.

My gut tugged, telling me to grab the tag, and without even thinking it through, I quickly unsnapped it from the handle of the suitcase and slipped it into my pocket.

"Maybe she'll leave if we stay back here," I heard Goddess Jillian say in a rushed voice.

It was perfect. I didn't need to stand around there any longer. They were on my list from Debbie, and they were moving to Lexington just after Debbie was murdered. Another coincidence I just couldn't accept.

Chapter Eleven

"What on earth happened to you?" I asked when Mazie walked up wearing a head scarf, jingling bracelets, and some sort of odd pendant around her neck.

"I had to buy all this crap from some psychic and Angela Ariel to even get them to talk to me about Debbie," she groaned underneath all the garb.

I doubled over in laughter.

"Don't take it off." I reached in my purse to get my phone. "I've got to get a picture of this."

"You better not." Mazie put her hand in front of her face.

"Too late." I was quicker than her and flipped it around to show her.

"You're evil." She laughed. "I do look so funny."

"They saw you coming a mile away and thought, look at that girl. She's going to buy whatever we say she needs." It was a trick Debbie Dually had pulled on me the second time I'd gone to see her.

Debbie had tried every which way for me to light incense all over the funeral home. I saw the reaction on

Hettie Bell's face yesterday when Debbie was flailing that feather all around the smoke.

"I did it all for you, Emma Lee Raines." Mazie pretended to pout. "Just because you're my friend, and I can't have you going to jail."

"Awwww. I love you too." I wanted her to know the feeling was mutual. "Get to the good stuff."

"Before I do that, did you find your people?" she asked.

Out of the corner of my eye, I noticed Fluggie Callahan walking down the aisle nearest to the exit.

"There's Fluggie," I pointed out.

"She must've gotten Mervin's name." Mazie was probably right. The more digging Fluggie did, the more she found out. I knew only because I'd seen her in action a few times.

"Let's get out of here." I motioned to the exit.

"Well? What did your people say?" she asked once we were outside.

"They are a couple who just so happen to have moved to Lexington recently." I pulled the luggage tag out of my pocket and handed it to her.

"You took a luggage tag?" she asked and looked at it. "Oh my God, Emma! This is great!" She squealed. "Mervin Dually and Deborah Holt! What luck!"

"What?" I ripped the tag out of her hand and read it, feeling dumbfounded. "Mervin Dually and Deborah Holt, 223 Cheshire Court, Lexington, KY."

"You found Debbie's ex," Mazie gasped with excitement on our way back to her car. "What are you going to do?"

"We are going to pay him a visit," I told her. "Not that he killed Debbie, but he can be checked out. What did you find out?"

"Warrioress Roma was a no-show, so they had some other person in her place that sold me this crystal thing." She lifted the pendant. "Something about little spirits liking the children's department at the library, and I don't need to take any home," she said and unlocked the car doors. "Then Angela Ariel, she was a bit odd. She said that she'd heard about Debbie this morning after she'd flew in from another convention in California."

"Was she really in California?" I asked, never assuming anything.

"Yep. I did a quick search on a database from the airlines. I'm technically not supposed to have access to it, and don't ask me how I do." She was firm with her words.

"Fine. Let's head on over to Debbie's house. I saw David leaving the convention. I wonder if he was there to see his father?" I put my hands in the air then buckled my seat belt. I took another look at the luggage tag and reread it, thinking about the dumb luck I'd just had.

"You better watch him." Debbie Dually appeared in the back seat. "He's got more moves than a Slinky going down an escalator."

"What? Is she here? Hi, Debbie!" Mazie was just too excited. "I'm so happy to be helping Emma get you to the other side."

"Chipper little thing," Debbie noted and grinned. "I like her."

"She likes you and how happy you are." I thought Mazie would love hearing how Debbie felt about her.

"More than happy." Mazie decided to go on a ten-minute talking spree to Debbie while I was left with my thoughts.

The thing I knew for sure was that out of the four names Debbie had given me, Jillian and Mervin were the only real suspects I could truly look into. Then there was the mystery guy on Debbie's answering machine who David had filed the police report on. I also couldn't forget all the clients Debbie claimed to be regulars and who rarely did what she asked.

My plan for the rest of the day was to visit with David and see where we stood, not to mention pick his brain about Mervin, find out where the mystery stalker guy lived and try to see him, then drive past Mervin's luggage tag address. Not that I'd stop there, but you never knew.

Since I'd become a snooping-around amateur-sleuth kind of gal, I'd learned you've got to go with the flow or at least where the ghosts take you. Not everything goes as planned. Like the convention. I found it interesting David was there.

"Hello?" I answered my phone when Jack Henry called.

"Good morning." He was always so chipper, and his slow southern drawl was music to my ears. "What are you doing this morning?"

"I'm working." It was only nine a.m., and if he knew I was with Mazie and we'd already been to the psychic convention and gotten some information before going to see David, he wouldn't be happy. "What are you doing?"

"I'm working in Lexington today." Okay... did he see us in Mazie's car? I jerked around and looked out all the windows. He kept talking.

"What?" Mazie asked in a low whisper. "Another ghost?"

I shook my head. It was ridiculous to think Jack Henry had seen us. Lexington was a bigger city, and there were plenty of places he could be other than where we were currently.

"What are you doing in Lexington?" I asked, knowing there wasn't a Kentucky State Police post there.

"Jack Henry? Lexington?" Mazie's eyes grew big. I put a finger up to my lips for her to stop talking. I'd realized that was sometimes hard for her. She was like one of those old windup toys—once you got her going, she had to be worn down. "Which way?" She asked for directions to Debbie and David's house.

I continued to give her finger directions while Jack Henry was on the phone.

"They are having a few drills on terrorist threats, and I've got to get my hours in. I called to make sure you were okay since I could tell you were a little mad last night when I asked you to stop snooping." Jack Henry was one of those guys that didn't like conflict. He never wanted us to fight or argue, but sometimes it was healthy. "You barely kissed me good night."

"I was tired. It's not every day I'm hauled down to the police station and accused of killing someone. I'm not upset. I love you and only want to make sure Trevor O'Neil finds the killer." I pointed at the next street for Mazie to turn and gave her numbers with my fingers to which house was theirs.

"Good. I thought since you don't have to do a funeral today, that we could meet at Bella Vino." He suggested our favorite little Italian restaurant. "You can drive to Lexington on my lunch break."

Mazie put the car in park at the curb in front of Debbie's house.

"What time is your lunch break?" I asked.

"Around noon," he said. I looked at my watch.

"Nine now." I rolled through all the places I needed to visit, which meant something was going to have to be put on the back burner because it would take me forty-five minutes to get back to Lexington to get my hearse and drive forty-five minutes back. "Sure. If I leave Sleepy Hollow by eleven fifteen, I should be fine."

Mazie moaned and groaned in the driver's seat to get my attention.

"I'll see you soon." I hung up the phone. "What? After last night, I have to stay on top of things and not let him think I'm doing any snooping. We are going to have to visit here with David and head back. We can do a drive by Debbie's ex's new house later this afternoon."

"Whatever. Let's go so we can hurry." Mazie acted a little hurt. She'd been working so hard on this case and wanted so desperately to be an honorary Betweener. It was sweet how she was acting.

She hurried out of the car, and I followed her to the door. Before I could knock, David swung it open and stood in the doorway.

"You see her, don't you?" David's eyes were hollow, black circles underneath. "I stayed up all night trying to get her to visit me. I was so desperate and out of my head, I went to see my own father and his fake psychic bride."

"Can we talk inside?" I asked him. There was a jingle behind me. I knew Debbie had come and didn't need to turn around. "I will tell you everything I know."

A sadness swept over me when I entered, taking my breath away. It didn't bother Mazie a bit. She strolled right on in and walked around Debbie's table, taking it all in.

"What are you doing?" David asked Mazie. "Stop touching my mother's things."

"It's okay. Tell him it's okay." Debbie stood as close to him as she could get.

"Your mom said it's okay." I offered him a sympathetic smile before I opened my arms to give him a hug. "I'm so sorry."

Like the little boy I'd met a few years ago, he melted into my arms. My heart ached. He might've been a college man now, but he was still too young to lose his mother.

"Can I get you some tea?" he asked, pulling away and wiping his tears. "I know my mom would've already had you a cup and not offered, but I'm still learning."

"We will show him." Debbie nodded. "I will teach you, and you will teach him." Debbie had a plan for David to learn.

"I'd love some tea while I tell you everything I know." I walked into the family room and tugged Mazie along with me, while we waited for David to make us tea. "But first

I'd like you to tell me about the guy who has been stalking your mom."

I reached into my bag and took out the pages Mazie had given me with the police report David had filed against him against his mom's wishes.

"I know it's probably not as good as Mom's." He was a little calmer than before. He put the tray on the coffee table, and we helped ourselves while he looked over the pages. "Kent Luebe. I gave his name to the Sleepy Hollow sheriff."

"Did you happen to know anything about his wife coming to see your mom?" I asked since Debbie clearly hadn't said too much about it.

"Natalia has been a weekly client of Mom's for years. Mom never got close to her like she did you. Natalia always questioned Mom when she was in the zone, bringing Mom out of the zone." He glanced into the room where Debbie did her work as though he were remembering something.

Debbie had floated in the room and sat down at the table like she did with her clients.

"I remember." Debbie ran a hand along the incense in the middle of the table. It wasn't unusual for Betweener clients to be in a transition period and not recall all the details of their living life. It could be very frustrating to me when I was trying to ask questions and figure out details of their murder or who might've been involved. "Natalia never wanted to believe me when I told her about Kent and his ways."

"His ways?" I asked.

"Mom?" David ran into the other room. "Mom, please tell me what I'm supposed to do? I know how to read people, but I'm not like you."

"His ways?" I talked over David's pleas. "David, please. I have to hear what she's saying."

Frustrated, David sat down in the chair across the table where Debbie's clients would sit and stared at her empty chair where her ghost was, only he couldn't see her.

Debbie continued when she could see that David was calmer.

"Kent was fired. He hadn't told her. She thought he was going to work every day. She came to me for financial advice. I told her there was no money coming in and Kent was no longer going to his job." Debbie's eyes were more than haunting—they held fright. "It was never written in the cards how she was going to leave him."

"Why has he been stalking you?" I questioned.

She pointed to the CDs on the shelf in the corner of the room where her crystals and extra items she needed were stacked. "Look for his name."

"She wants me to find the CDs with Kent's name on them," I said to David.

He didn't waste any time. He jumped up and grabbed a stack. Recording a session was an extra cost to the client, and I'd never had mine recorded because I didn't want any sort of evidence I was a Betweener.

"Here." He handed me the stack.

We thumbed through them as quickly as we could. There were at least ten of them.

"I've got to go soon," I told them and looked at my watch. I was going to be cutting it close to meet Jack Henry. "Do you mind if I take these and bring them back?"

"Only if you tell me about my mom coming to visit before she was murdered like you said you would do," David reminded me.

All of us headed back into the family room, and I put the CDs in my crossbody bag.

"Your mom came to see me and insisted I confirm I was a Betweener." It was nice that I didn't have to explain my gift and that David completely understood what I meant. "I haven't had a client in a while, so when I continued to ask her why, she was upset. I don't think she wanted me to know she knew her own death was coming and that she was going to be murdered."

"How did she know?" He sucked in a couple of quick breaths as though he were trying to gain composure.

"I was reading someone's cards, and I saw it in their cards." Debbie had drifted into the room.

"Whose cards? Kent's? Someone else's?" I asked while I watched more and more of her living memories come back to her. "Maybe they had something to do with it. I mean," I spoke to her and forgot about the others in the room. "Tell me," I told her when she looked away from me. "Who was it?"

"Mervin." Her words washed over me. I could feel the color drain from my face.

"Your ex?"

"My husband." Those words did me in. "I'm not sure how he found me in Kentucky."

"Emma?" David was huddled over me when I came to. "Are you okay?"

"Emma Lee?" I rolled my eyes up toward the back of my head when heard Jack Henry. "Get her some water."

My head was in Jack Henry's lap, and he was rubbing my face with a cold washcloth.

"I'm sorry," Mazie apologized, crouching down next to me with a glass of water in her hand. "I didn't know what to do when you passed out. I grabbed your phone and called Jack Henry."

"Here." Jack Henry tilted my head and put the glass up to my lips.

I took a drink before grabbing the glass out of his hand and gulping it down.

"I was thirsty." I licked my lips and pushed myself up to sit. "I'm sorry. I don't know what…" I stopped talking when I remembered what had happened. "Your mom and dad aren't divorced," I blurted out and looked at David. "She said your dad came to see her and she read his cards or something like that." The details were a little fuzzy. "But then she admitted she saw her own death in his cards and that they weren't exes."

"That's it." Jack Henry stood up. "We are leaving, and I'm going to have Zula Fae keep an eye on you."

"No, you're not." I shook a finger at Jack Henry. "I'm tired of you telling me what I can and can't do. Here are your choices." I had to find out if Mervin killed Debbie. There was no turning back for me at this point. "You can either go to Mervin's house and check it out with me and Mazie, or I'm going without you. You can walk out that door right now and pretend you never heard this." I looked at Mazie. "If I ever pass out again, don't you dare call anyone. Not even if my heart stops. Got it?"

"Yeah. Got it." Mazie's voice cracked.

"Geez, Emma Lee." Jack Henry started to pace. He ran his hands through his hair and gnawed on his lip like he did when he was trying to figure out a crime.

"Did you say my dad and mom aren't divorced?" David's face was blank. "He has a house here?" He questioned with a hurt tone.

"Oh, David," Debbie sobbed. "I never wanted him to know. I was going to give his dad a divorce, but they continued to use my name, and we were working toward a deal."

"Your name? A deal?" I asked Debbie. Everyone turned to see the empty space I was talking to. "Now you have to give me the details. I can't keep chasing these simple clues when you could tell me the answers."

"All I know is Goddess Jillian is not her name. Her real name is Deborah Holt. She's a young show pony Mervin conned into thinking they could have a good life together if they pretended to be psychic. He told her how I made a good living at it." Debbie made me think back to the convention center.

"That's why the real psychics came out to greet me when I passed. They knew my gift, but Goddess What's-her-fake-name and Mervin didn't even know I was standing in their booth." I patted my pants pockets. "Where's the luggage tag?" I asked Mazie when I didn't remember where I'd put it then looked at my watch.

"It's in the car. Do you want me to go get it?" she asked.

"No. It's not even noon, and they'll be at the convention until seven tonight. We are going to check out their place." I wasn't about to waste any more time.

"Emma." Jack Henry's voice was stern. "No. You're not. That's illegal."

"It's only illegal if I get caught."

The knock at the door made us all jump.

"I have a client," David informed us and went to the door to let them in. As he ushered them into the room to the right, we headed out the door.

"I'll be back," I told him and gave him a quick hug.

"Emma, I'm telling you that you can't do this." Jack ran alongside of me.

"You can't tell me what to do." I got into Mazie's car, and she drove off with Jack Henry standing on the curb.

Chapter Twelve

223 Cheshire Court wasn't the slightest bit hard to find since it was about a mile from Debbie's house. Jack Henry had called me several times during the couple-of-minute drive and stood outside of the passenger door as soon as Mazie put the car in park.

"I'm going to arrest you." Jack Henry's bogus threats didn't bother me.

"You couldn't stand the thought of Trevor taking me in for questioning, so I know you aren't going to arrest me." I tapped him lightly on the nose. "Besides, you're too cute in that outfit."

Jack Henry didn't have on his standard French gray state trooper uniform. Instead he wore a blue pair of pants with a blue short-sleeved collared shirt with the Kentucky logo on the pocket. It was the uniform troopers wore when they had classes or were on desk duty.

Mazie had already gotten out of the car and headed around the house before I even got around Jack Henry.

"Hurry," Mazie whispered in a louder voice than she should've from the open front door. "The back door's unlocked."

"See, not breaking and entering." I scooted around Jack Henry and his big sigh, but he was tight on my heels.

"What are you looking for? A written confession?" he asked. "So what if they were still married."

"I'm looking for cyanide, in case you want to help." I stopped before I walked into the front door and turned around. "I warn you, if you walk through this door, you are aiding and abetting."

"Funny." Jack Henry didn't look amused at my joke and headed in before me. He took a quick glance around the room where there were nothing but boxes. By the looks of it, they hadn't attempted to unpack anything.

I followed behind him into another room full of boxes that connected to a kitchen. There was coffee in the coffeepot that was cold to the touch. There were a few flyers about the psychic convention lying on the counter but nothing else.

Mazie and I stood there, not really knowing what to do.

"I know what to look for. Why do you think Mervin did it?" Jack Henry fired off questions and plucked gloves from his back pocket, handing them to me. "Don't look at me like that. I'm covering us all."

After we'd all put the gloves on, we started to open up the kitchen drawers and walk around separately. I went back into the room where the front door was located and opened a couple of boxes that appeared to be only clothes.

"Debbie didn't say he did it. I'm having a hard time getting anything out of her other than wanting me to help David with his gift before we do find out who her killer is." My voice projected into the other room.

It made we wonder if she was sabotaging the entire case just so she did have time with David.

"He's been wanting this divorce for years, according to the date on the papers. For some reason, Debbie didn't give it to him," I said. "I'm not sure how he found out she was living in Lexington after she left Florida. She doesn't know either. It was one of the last things I remember her saying before I passed out."

"That isn't necessarily a reason for him to have killed her." Jack Henry was always the voice of 'good cop' and tried to go by the principle that someone was innocent until proven guilty.

"Guys." Mazie stood in the hallway, looking into a room. "Ummm."

Jack Henry didn't wait for Mazie to say anything else. He was already in the room taking photos with his phone camera, then he was on the phone.

"Trevor, this is Deputy Jack Henry Ross." Jack Henry stepped outside of the room to finish up his conversation with Trevor.

My stomach hurt at the sight of all the photos of Debbie Dually hanging on the wall. They'd been altered. Some had hand-drawn daggers to her eyes, while others had them on her neck. There were a few articles from the *Lexington Herald Leader* about Debbie that were also hanging up. There was one written by our very own Fluggie Callahan, who used to work at the Herald before she moved to Sleepy Hollow.

"This sure looks like someone who has a beef with someone." I took my phone out of my pocket and scrolled through the contacts to find Fluggie's number.

"It looks like a killer's trophy wall to me." Mazie was right. The wall was filled with photos of Debbie and

Goddess Jillian. "Is Debbie here? It sure looks like Mervin Dually was trying to turn Deborah Holt into Debbie Dually."

"No. She's not here. And I think you're right." I shook my head and wondered if she was going to come back to face her killer. Her ex. Betweener clients rarely stuck around after I'd help find their killer. They generally were ready to move to the other side. Sometimes they'd linger to say goodbye or have a message for a loved one. If I knew Debbie, her love for David wouldn't let her cross until she left him a message with me.

"You callin' to give me that interview?" Fluggie answered her phone in a hopeful voice.

"Nope. I've called to ask you if you know a Mervin Dually?" I asked her.

"I might've done a little work for him." Her words tied Mervin to the Lexington area and how he found Debbie.

"What sort of work?" I asked.

"Does this have to do with his ex-wife's murder?" she asked. There was a lingering silence between us. I wanted something from her, and she wanted something from me. Both of us would benefit. It would tell me exactly how Mervin got here and why. I would be giving her a scoop to write up for tomorrow's paper. "What if I wait for forty-eight hours to publish whatever it is on the internet?"

Fluggie only published a printed version of the *Sleepy Hollow News* once a week but updated the online version daily and as news came in.

"Fine. Mervin Dually has moved to Lexington. I've got a source who told me he had found Debbie here because they weren't divorced. My source also revealed there is some sort of trophy wall in his house. He'd kept an article written by you." The silence on the other end was eerie.

"I wrote an article on the psychic convention and interviewed some of them. Debbie didn't give me her name. She simply offered her services. He called the paper, wanting to talk to me. He said Debbie was his ex-wife and was very happy for her. He said he had some of her items she'd left behind and wanted to ship them to her. I told him I had no idea where she lived but would be happy to get them to her if he shipped them to me. He shipped the boxes, and I took them to her. That's how I got to know her and see her as a client." Her voice cracked. "I had no idea he moved here. I never heard from him since."

"He's done more than moved here." I glanced at one of the folders on the desk in that room. "I think he killed Debbie."

The other end of the phone was dead silent, and so was the entire car ride back to Sleepy Hollow, with Mazie driving and Jack Henry in the back.

"I'm sorry, but if we are right, you'll be taken off leave in no time." I knew my words weren't going to make Jack Henry any less mad about Trevor calling the head of the state police and telling him how Jack Henry had unlawfully broken into a house and impeded an investigation. As a result, Jack Henry was placed on leave until further notice.

"Emma Lee, I knew it was wrong and should've called the police to stop you myself." Jack Henry didn't even look at me. He stared out the window.

"I have some good news," Mazie said in a chipper voice, though she didn't make the atmosphere any better. "While you two were talking to the police, I got an email on my phone from the library in Cincinnati. They've been interviewing for a new head librarian for their downtown branch, and I applied. They had me come up for an interview. I thought I bombed it, but apparently, I'm exactly what they are looking for."

"Mazie! That's wonderful." I couldn't help but be thrilled for her since it was such a big step up from little Sleepy Hollow. "Are you going to take it?"

"Yes. Of course I am. I leave in a week." She rambled on and on about how she was going to be going back and forth for a while.

My thoughts were in my stomach with my heart. Not only was I losing a real friend, I couldn't help but feel like I was also losing my boyfriend.

Chapter Thirteen

"I saw you coming down the street." Cheryl Lynn Doyle scooted a cup of coffee across the counter when I walked into Higher Ground. "I made it extra strong. I heard you've had a day."

"You heard?" My left eyebrow rose when I knew she meant the gossip had already started to circulate.

"Yeah. Fluggie Callahan was in here when one of the sheriff's deputies came in here looking for her." Cheryl Lynn leaned on the counter with her forearms flat across the glass. "They took her in for questioning. They said something about her article about Debbie or something like that and how they'd taken a man and woman into custody."

I knew she was talking about Mervin and Deborah Holt. Trevor had called it in to have them picked up at the psychic convention before he let us drive back to Sleepy Hollow.

Cheryl Lynn pointed back to one of the fancy coffee machines behind her. "Zula and Ernest were in here getting a fancy coffee." She smiled. "I couldn't hear over the machine."

"Granny was on a date." I didn't want to talk about the investigation of Debbie's murder. My spirits were low, and talking about Granny made me feel better. "She had a latte?"

I'd never seen Granny drink anything but tea. She rarely drank coffee and many times tried to get me to switch to hot tea. No thank you.

"I could tell." Cheryl Lynn smiled. "They were so cute. It was like old-fashioned dating. They came in. He pulled out the café chair, and she sat down. He came up to the counter and ordered for her."

"Granny let him?" I couldn't believe it. Granny was so independent, and I couldn't even see her letting him pull out her chair, though she wanted that type of relationship for me.

"Oh yeah." Cheryl Lynn's chin slowly rose up and then down. "He even scooted his chair next to her." Cheryl Lynn let out a long romantic sigh and gazed out the window. "Where are those type of guys now?"

"I have no idea." I shook my head and took a couple of sips out of the mug.

"How about a vanilla-glazed gingerbread cookie? Fresh out of the oven."

I glanced over her shoulders at the cooling rack where the cookies were waiting to be plated and put into the glass bakery case.

"I will have one." My mouth watered looking at them.

"I thought something else was going on." Cheryl plated a few cookies and scooted around the counter, passing me and setting the plate on the small café table next to the counter. "I'm not busy. Let's talk. What's wrong? You should be really happy the sheriff has someone in custody and you're off the hook."

"I know, but it wasn't like they stumbled upon the information for investigating." I shoved the entire cookie in my mouth and watched Cheryl's eyes grow big.

"Are you telling me you were at it again?" I knew her question was pointed at my bad habit of snooping. "Emma," she gasped and grabbed one of the cookies off the plate, putting it in her mouth.

"It's worse than that. I can handle the heat when I do something illegal to make something right, but Jack Henry was with me and in one of his Kentucky State Police uniforms." I knew it wasn't coming out the way I wanted it to because Cheryl Lynn looked so confused. "I know it's out of Jack Henry's character, but I wasn't listening to him about sneaking into Debbie's husband's house. He followed me there and wouldn't let me go without him."

"Aww… and we thought romance was dead," she purred, her shoulders lifted toward her ears.

"Yes. It's dead. That's where we found the new evidence, and he did the right thing and called Trevor. I would've done an anonymous call, but not him. Always by the book." My eyes filled with tears.

"Are you saying he got in trouble?"

"Trouble? Off the force until further notice." Hearing the actual words come out of my mouth made me so sick to my stomach, the gingerbread cookies were no longer appealing to me.

"I'm assuming he's really mad, and that's what wrong." She reached over and patted my hand. "Oh, honey. I'm so sorry."

The bell over the door dinged, and we both turned to look.

It was a customer for her and a client for me. Debbie Dually was standing outside the window looking in at me. She ghosted across the street and over to the sidewalk as though she were heading to Eternal Slumber.

"I'll see you later." I got up so Cheryl could help the customer.

"Let me know if you need anything. I'm always here." I knew her words were sincere, and that made me feel good since I knew my true good friend, Mazie, was about to leave me.

I checked my phone for any calls or texts from Jack Henry, but there was nothing. Debbie's ghost looked back at me a couple of times to see if I was following. Was this the last time I was going to see her? Was this the meeting where she'd give me her final instructions before she headed up to the great beyond?

"Emma Lee, your granny has lost her mind, and I'm not going to stand for it. I thought you were crazy all these years, but I think it's her, and you need to make her an appointment immediately." Doc Clyde came out of nowhere. His pointy chin stuck out under his pouty lips.

I'd never seen that man move so quickly.

"Doc Clyde." I put my hand up to my chest. "You scared me to death. I think I need to be checked out for a heart attack."

"I'm not joking. You think this is a joke?" He put his hand on my arm to stop me.

"I'm in a real rush. Can we talk about Granny another time?" I watched beyond him as Debbie's ghost stopped right in front of the funeral home. I knew I had limited time before the Betweener clients had to move on and Debbie really needed to talk to me.

"No, *we cannot.*" He acted as though I didn't have a say in the matter. "That woman broke my heart. Her going around wanting to be a doctor's wife, and when I proposed, she was happy. I mean really happy."

"Aww." I patted his arm. "You know Granny. Give her time. You've just got to hang in there like a hair in a biscuit."

"You think so, because she was drinking a latte with that darn lawyer. A latte, Emma Lee." Poor Doc's mouth was quivering.

"I'll see what I can find out." I waved at him over my shoulder, leaving him standing there with a broken heart. "Dang," I said to myself. "Granny can bag four men in her lifetime, and I can't seem to hang on to one."

The thought about Jack Henry was unsettling, and I knew I'd have to go see him at some point if he wasn't going to contact me.

"Hey, John Howard," I greeted the town handyman and my gravedigger. He did a few things around Eternal Slumber, mostly lawn work and landscaping, but today he was taking down the folded chairs in the viewing room where Purdy Ford had been laid out. "Thank you so much for taking those down."

"The banker came to see you today." John Howard was smart enough to know what it was about without me telling him. "He left some papers with me. I put them on your desk."

"Thanks," I grumbled, knowing I was late on this month's business loan. I had to take out the loan after Charlotte Rae had died so I could buy the entire business. The cancellations' connection to me being tied to Debbie's murder didn't help matters.

"Emma Lee, I'm real worried about Bea Allen." John Howard never expressed any sort of concern for anyone as long as I'd known him. "I was down at the courthouse pulling weeds from the cracks in the sidewalk when I overheard Bea Allen and O'Dell discussing the funeral business."

"I'm listening." I walked into the room with him. I picked up the stack of chair covers and put them in the cleaning bag he'd started so we could get them down to the dry cleaners in case someone did come back to Eternal Slumber now that I was no longer a suspect in Debbie's case.

Speaking of Debbie…

"You know what, I've got to do something really fast." I pushed the coverings in the bag so it would pack down. "Can we talk about this in about twenty minutes?"

"Yeah. I guess." He looked perplexed. "But I think you need to hear what…"

"I will in a little bit," I called over my shoulder.

Whatever he had to say about the Burnses could wait. Nothing they did was pressing to me, and I wasn't about to lose these precious, last few minutes I had with Debbie.

I hurried back to my office, thinking Debbie was there. When she wasn't, I looked in Charlotte's old office, and when she wasn't there, I headed to my apartment, where I found her in my family room.

"There you are." I gave her a good once-over so I could remember her. "Well, I'm ready to learn how to help David."

"You're a good friend, Emma Lee. I'd never had a client who was a Betweener, and it thrilled me to know you embraced your gift." Debbie waved the feather in front of the smoldering incense. "David is a good boy. Man. He's going to be fine. I want him to finish his college. He will be able to help people better that way."

"He really wants to take over your business." It made me remember the CDs I'd taken from her house that I needed to give back now that Mervin was in custody. "He thinks he can do well."

"He will use his gift later in life, and his gift will help him do the right thing to achieve his purpose." She confused me.

"But I thought…" I blinked a few times trying to wrap my head around how I was going to tell him this, so I asked. "What do you want me to say to him?"

"Exactly what I just told you." She floated around my family room, swiping the feather into the smoke, forcing it into the corners of the walls.

"Is it time?" I asked when I felt like she was creating a smoke tunnel to help her cross to the other side. "I want you to know how much you helped me. When Jack Henry first made the appointment with you about my gift, I was a mess. I thought I was nuts and the medication Doc Clyde had me on made me sad. You changed my life. I'll never forget how much you made me feel normal and helped me to embrace my gift."

"Thank you." Debbie smiled. "Now, can you go catch my killer because I'm ready to move on."

"Your killer?" A nervous laugh escaped me. "Mervin killed you."

"Lordy no. Mervin couldn't kill an ant." Debbie ghosted away. "The killer is still out there."

Chapter Fourteen

"Still out here? Not crossed over?" Mazie asked from the stack of papers on the floor in her office in the library. "Are you sure?"

"She's right out there, in the reference section." Debbie had showed up in the hearse on my way over to see Mazie and followed me into the library.

I looked out into the library and saw Debbie's ghost had moved next to John Howard Lloyd.

My mind was so jumbled with knowing that Debbie's killer was still out there, the wrong persons were in custody, and I was going to have to tell David he wasn't to be a psychic. This was not how I saw this little Betweener client situation going down at all. "When I solve their murders, they go away," I mumbled. "I'll be right back. I think John Howard wants to talk to me."

John Howard greeted me with a toothless smile when I approached him. "Emma Lee."

"John Howard, are you following me?" I asked.

"No, ma'am," he grunted and looked down at his shoes. "I was coming in here to get a cup of coffee."

"I have all the coffee you want at the funeral home." I didn't believe him. There was something going on with him, and I'd seen him behave like this one other time.

When Bea Allen Burns stole him from me as an employee, it took me some fancy accounting work to get him back, and I sure hoped it wasn't happening again. That's why I didn't press him on why he was really here.

"Okay." I smiled. "I'll see you tomorrow."

He nodded and walked around me to head back to the coffee stand Mazie had set up near the computers as a complimentary offering to the library guests.

"What about Kent?" Mazie smacked her hands together. "We never listened to the CDs because we thought Mervin did it."

"You're right. Problem," I groaned and dug down into my bag where I'd stuck the CDs in there. I took out a stack. "I don't have a CD player."

"The library has several." Mazie wiggled her brows in excitement and pushed up to stand. "They are in storage, but I'll get them."

Mazie went to retrieve the ancient compact disc player, and I took my phone from my pocket. I clicked my favorites button from the call screen and clicked on the only name on there.

Jack Henry.

"Hi," was all I could think of when he did answer. I was a little surprised. "I love you. We have a problem."

"We have several problems." He wasn't talking about the murder; he was talking about us. "I know we started dating when we found out you were a Betweener. I love that you can help people. I adore it, actually. You're sensitive and caring. It's another thing when it hurts people you love."

"Jack, I didn't force you to go into Mervin's house. You insisted," I blurted out when I knew I should've just agreed and moved on. I put my hand over my mouth and the phone, whispering, "That's not why I called. Not that it makes a difference to your situation, but Mervin didn't kill Debbie. She's still here."

The silence on the other end of the phone reminded me of the first time I did tell Jack Henry about me seeing ghosts. The memory ruffled through my mind. It actually made me smile.

"It'll take Trevor a day or so to go through all of Mervin's information, which will buy some time." Was

Jack Henry on my side? I sat there trying to analyze what he'd said. "Emma Lee?"

"I'm here. I'm trying to process what you just said." Instead of trying to figure it out, I waited to see his response.

"I've got nothing else to do."

"Oh, Jack Henry!" I couldn't help but get excited about the fact Jack Henry was going to help me, and I knew he was going to do anything to help. "Where do we start?"

Mazie walked back into the office with an old CD player. I grabbed a piece of paper off her desk and wrote down "Jack Henry." She nodded and started to thumb through the CDs.

"I've already started." Of course he had. "You told me David had gone to the psychic convention. I wanted to know why he went there. Was it because he wanted to try to connect with his mom? Did he know his dad was there? Did he even know about his dad? So I called David."

Mazie held up the CD she'd settled on. There was a date on it from a week ago.

"Most recent," she whispered, shrugging her shoulders, and took the CD out of the protective sleeve. She fiddled with the CD player while I finished my conversation with Jack Henry.

"Did he answer?" I asked Jack Henry about his phone call to David.

"Yeah. He said he went there because he'd went through his mom's papers, and there was a note from Mervin. He wanted to talk to Debbie at the convention since they both were going to be there. When he went to see Mervin, Mervin seemed happy that Debbie was dead because it made their divorce final. Only…" I could hear the worry in Jack Henry's voice. "He did tell David he was entitled to half of Debbie's things."

I gasped.

"What?" Mazie jerked up and looked at me.

"Mervin told David he's entitled to half of what she had because they weren't divorced." I couldn't believe it.

"That's not true!" Debbie ghosted into the library office. "He is a freeloader. He's got Deborah Holt pretending to be psychic. He saw how much money I was making with my gift, and he's such a con, he's going to try to fool people."

"Is she here?" Mazie must've seen me focusing on the empty space in front of her.

"Yes." I nodded. "I understand that, but you didn't sign the divorce papers."

"Cool." Mazie plugged in a pair of earphones into the CD player and put them on.

"Emma, are you talking to Debbie?" Jack Henry asked from the other end of the phone.

"Emma Lee, whose side are you on?" Debbie growled. "You wouldn't tell me you're a Betweener before I was murdered, and now you want help so David keeps what is rightfully his?"

"That's not fair. I'm more than happy to get you to the other side, but I can't manipulate the law with the undone stuff you left behind." I didn't answer Jack Henry because I was afraid Debbie would leave if I didn't continue to talk to her. "I'll help David out in any way I can, but I've got to help you get crossed over."

"Then do your job!" she yelled, fanning the smoke my way before she stepped into a big plume of it and disappeared.

"Emma? What's wrong?" Jack Henry's tone held concern.

"I'm not sure what kind of help we are going to get from Debbie here on out." I gnawed on my bottom lip. "She insists I have to help David keep all her money."

"Do you know how much money she has?" Jack Henry asked.

"Not a clue, but she lived simply, and it only cost thirty-five dollars to see her for an hour, so I'm assuming not much." It was simple observation.

"She's squirreled away a huge 401(k). I'll probably get caught, and I'm prepared for it, but I used my credentials to make a few phone calls to someone I know in the IRS. I gave him Debbie's social, and she's got over one million dollars in her account." Jack Henry dropped a bomb on me.

My jaw dropped. To. The. Floor!

"Wa… wa… wa…" I stammered over my words. "One million dollars." I finally got it out. "Debbie has a 401(k) worth one million dollars."

"Yes. If she's still here, and Mervin didn't kill her, he sure will get some of that." Jack Henry's voice faded out.

"Emma!" Mazie ripped the earphones off her head. "Kent Luebe threatened to kill Debbie. And I don't think he knew she was taping him."

"Did she just say someone threatened to kill Debbie?" Jack Henry asked.

"She's listening to the CDs. I didn't know the full details because I've been talking to you." Kent definitely could be the killer, especially since he'd been stalking her and unhappy with what Debbie had done to his marriage.

"Emma Lee, meet me at Eternal Slumber with the CDs so I can hear them. I've got to grab this phone call from my mom. See you soon." He clicked off the phone.

His mother.

"What? Your face just went white." Mazie looked around the room like there was another ghost or something there.

"Jack Henry is taking a phone call from his mother." The thought of him telling her he'd been let go from the Kentucky State Police after she'd driven him crazy for a couple of years to take the job. "He wants to meet me at Eternal Slumber with the CDs because he's going to help figure out who killed Debbie."

When he didn't take the offer to join the force when they initially offered it to him, his mom blamed me for keeping him here, and it didn't establish a great relationship between us. She tolerated me, and I was overly nice to her.

"We can't worry about her." Mazie grabbed up the CDs and handed me the CD player. "You go meet him and figure this out. Get Debbie to the other side before I have to leave town."

Chapter Fifteen

You're going to call Natalia and tell her you were wrong. Kent Luebe's voice made me physically shake as the images of how frightened Debbie must've been when he would approach her flashed before me. *You tell her that I've had a job and I can provide for her. You made her leave me, and if you don't tell her how much I love her and do some sort of fake voodoo crap you do and tell her she'll die if she doesn't come back to me, I'll kill you.*

Jack Henry hit the back button.

I'll kill you. Jack Henry replayed it again and again. *I'll kill you. I'll kill you.*

"We've got to find this man." Panic rioted deep within me as the tears sat on the edge of my eyelids.

331 Downhair Road, said a faint whisper from the recording.

"What was that? Did you hear that?" I asked Jack Henry.

He rewound it.

331 Downhair Road. It sounded like one of those recordings you'd hear on the *Ghost Hunters* show where a ghost saying something was picked up but was a little skewed.

"I think it's Debbie giving an address." I grabbed my phone off the desk and punched in the address on my maps app. "It's in Lexington." I turned the phone around.

Jack Henry walked straight over to my computer and pulled up the Internet. He typed until he hit enter.

"If this is a lead, you and I are going to find it because it's your ticket to get off leave." I rubbed Jack Henry on the back, trying to make this easier for him. "Not only do I want Debbie to cross over, I want you to get your job back."

It was hard for me to say that since I really wanted him here back in Sleepy Hollow full-time, but the Kentucky State Police had been a dream for him. Not to mention his mother. Jo Francis Ross wasn't my biggest fan since Jack Henry had turned down the first job the state police had offered because we were dating.

When this second time came around, I knew it had to be in his cards if he had another chance. Plus, if we had a future, I did want Jo Francis to like me somewhat. That's when I'd encouraged Jack Henry to take the job, and we'd do the long-distance thing. It wasn't too bad, though my selfish self really wanted him with me... all the time.

"I'm not too worried about my job. I'm worried about you." He looked up at me with those deep brown eyes, making my heart melt down into my toes. "I've put the address in a database. It'll give me some history."

He glanced next to my computer while he waited for the three dots rolling across the monitor to pop up the results. He picked up the piece of paper from the bank. "What's this?"

"Nothing. I'm a little late on this month's payment, but it'll be fine." I gulped, knowing I just left it there like it was going to take care of itself. "I'll take care of it today. With everything going on, I haven't had time to take it there."

I took it from him and put it in another pile, trying to cover up the real reason I'd not paid it. It was all going to be okay. I knew as soon as we got this Debbie Dually murder wrapped up, the clients who left, like the Clarks, would come back to Eternal Slumber for their final resting arrangements. The Clarks were on my list to go see since I was no longer a suspect. At least, I didn't think I was.

The computer beeped, and the results popped up. A photo of a man and all of his statistics came up. The sound of jingles told me Debbie was on her way.

"That's Kent Luebe." Debbie appeared behind Jack Henry. "He's a bad man."

"Did he know you were taping him?" I asked her and decided not to even bring up earlier, when she ghosted away.

"No." She put her nose in the smoke of the incense. "I don't understand why I can't remember everything, but I feel like you're getting close."

There was a knock at the office door. Debbie ghosted away.

"What's going on here?" Sheriff Trevor O'Neil stood at the door. His eyes shifted between me and Jack Henry. "I saw your patrol car out there and thought I'd stop in to tell you personally how sorry I am they put you on leave."

His eyes darted to the computer monitor. I quickly hit the off key to turn it off but not the computer.

"Yeah, well, you could've handled it a little differently." Jack Henry wasn't pleased and didn't make it any more pleasant for Trevor. "If that's all you wanted, then you can go."

"Just so you know, Mervin Dually and Deborah Holt checked out. They had alibis with witnesses, and there wasn't any trace of cyanide." Trevor shook his head. "In fact, the two went right over to the courthouse after we let them go and applied for a marriage license. Said they were going to get hitched as soon as he had a death certificate for Debbie."

"That was fast," Debbie said as she swept back into the room. "He was never one to be alone."

I gulped and tried not to look her way.

"That was fast." I sighed and turned back around so Trevor would get the hint that I wasn't going to give him the time of day

"Emma Lee." Trevor cleared his throat. I turned back around to face him. "I know you or someone with you already went to the psychic convention so if you found out anything about the case, I suggest you tell me. I can't nab you on the murder, yet." He paused. "But if I find out you had some information, you can be arrested."

"Thanks, Trevor." Jack Henry stood up.

The two men stood solid as oak trees as they stared across the room at each other before Jack Henry went back to the chair and sat down with his back to Trevor.

Trevor let himself out.

"He's a jerk," I said to Jack Henry and flipped the monitor back on.

"It looks like our man Kent has been in a little trouble before, and I can stop by for a little visit to make sure he's kept his nose clean." Jack Henry was sly. "I can also throw it in there about Debbie."

"Great. I'll grab my bag." I started to go over to the credenza to gather my things to go with him, but he grabbed my wrist.

"I think I need to do this alone." Jack Henry's grip told me he meant business.

"But I have to see for myself. If Debbie shows up, I can ask him questions and her questions to ask him." This was how the Betweener gig worked.

"You heard Trevor." Jack Henry's voice was stern. "He said that if he finds out you've withheld any information, you'll be arrested. It's a matter of time before they get through all of Debbie's client list and figure out this guy had a beef with her after they talk to Natalia."

"Now what?" I asked with a little annoyance in my voice when there was a slight knock at the door. I figured it was Trevor. "Mr. Peabody, come in."

Mr. Peabody was standing at the door with his briefcase in his hand.

"I've come with some good news." There was a little giddyup in his step. "I took Zula Fae out for coffee, and we had a good time. Sort of a second date."

Was that his good news? I didn't dare burst his bubble and tell him that I already knew.

"I'm a bit worried about Doc Clyde." Mr. Peabody sat down in a chair and made himself comfortable. I didn't say a word about Doc Clyde stopping me on the street. "He's been sending her flowers and chocolates." Mr. Peabody's brows furrowed. "How can I compete with all that?"

"Didn't you two bake?" I asked about the advice I'd already given him.

"We did." He nodded. "I learned how to make apple popovers."

"Her recipe?" I asked when I thought he was going to teach her to make his recipes, and he confirmed. "You need to tell her that you're making your recipes so she can see you have your own skills in the kitchen."

Jack Henry continued to look around on the computer.

"I'll do that." He got up and headed to the door. "Oh, before I forget and the reason I stopped by." He paused and dug down into his briefcase. "You're no longer a suspect in the death of Debbie Dually, but they did tell me to let you know they are serious about charges if you are keeping anything from them about the investigation. I've got your statement here."

"Thank you for stopping by. I really appreciate all you have done for me." I walked over and took the papers he dug out. "I'll be sure to put in a good word for Granny."

He nodded a couple of times and went on his way.

"It's official." I read the papers as I walked back to Jack Henry.

"And this is why I'm insisting you don't come with me." His face was still and his eyes sharp. "I'm already on leave, and I can handle what they say to me or throw at me because I know ways around it."

"But…" I started to protest and met with a look that told me he was not going to budge. "Fine."

Chapter Sixteen

In no way, shape, or form was I happy about Jack Henry going to visit my lead in the case without me, but I also knew I had other people to see like Bea Allen Burns, go to the bank, and stop by the Clarks to see if they'd change their minds about changing their preneed arrangements from Burns.

I quickly updated my notes about Debbie's murder and marked two of the three suspects off, Mervin Dually and Deborah Holt, leaving Kent Luebe as my last resort.

"Emma Lee," Debbie said my name from the corner of the room. "You've got company." She made her way to the door before anyone was there and fanned the smoke around the edges as though she was cleansing the person before they walked in, making me a little anxious.

Jo Francis Ross, Jack Henry's mom, was suddenly standing at the office door.

She had on leopard flats, a white button-down tucked into a pair of skinny black pants, and a large silver beaded scarf tied around her neck. Her dark hair cascaded down her shoulders, long and straight with a full body that made me envious.

Jo Francis had on the latest trends. She was the cool mom when we were growing up. Cool as in having the svelte mom body with the clothes to match. The creepy funeral home girl's mom, my mom, was not a trendsetter in fashion nor career choice, and Jo Francis didn't see my career as a great one either.

"Emma Lee, I've come to talk to you." She entered without me agreeing to have the time, but I did take a little pleasure in the dog hair on her pants.

She had two labs, Bolt and Rocky, who she adored, so I knew if she loved animals, she wasn't all that bad. Plus, she loved Jack Henry with every fiber of her being, which made her so protective, and I did appreciate how much she cared for him, though it was at my expense sometimes.

"It'll only take a minute." She stopped right in front of my desk and clasped her hands in front of her. Her purse dangled from her bent elbow. "I understand you're once again in a little pickle." She raised her perfect brows.

"Any charges against me were dropped." I reached behind me next to the computer to get the paper Mr. Peabody had dropped off.

"No. I'm not talking about that." She unsnapped the purse and took something out, unfolding it. "Though I did hear about that too." She rolled her eyes, which told me she was holding back and Jack Henry had probably threatened her somehow. "I was at Higher Grounds and heard a little chatter from that awful Bea Allen Burns."

I groaned.

"I have to accept the fact my son is and will always be in your favor even though you've seen a little trouble." She had such a hard time complimenting me, but I'd take what I could get from her. "And that granny of yours." She tugged her lips closed as if she needed to stop herself from flapping her mouth. She simply stuck the piece of paper in my face. "This should help."

"Two hundred and fifty thousand dollars?" I blinked at the check she was holding in her hand. "What is this?"

"Bea Allen was telling that awful Beulah Paige something about Eternal Slumber being in financial trouble and soon Burns would be the only funeral home in Sleepy Hollow." She jutted the check in front of me like she wanted me to take it. "I'm not sure what your future is with my son, but I know he'd want us to help you."

The Rosses had money. Jack Henry grew up far different from me. He'd had a luxurious life, which horses and tobacco farming offered. Jo Francis had been an interior decorator for years and made good money from that.

"I can't." I resisted the urge to jump up and grab her into a big bear hug. This was the first time she seemed to have accepted me, albeit through money, but it was her way. "Does Jack Henry know?"

"He doesn't know that I'm giving you money if that's what you're asking." Her lashes flew up, and her eyes narrowed. "You haven't told him about your financial issues, have you?"

She placed the check on the desk when she realized my little secret.

"No." I looked at the check and couldn't help but think how much that would help.

"Then," she brushed her hands together. "This will be our little secret."

"I can't," I protested, pushing the check back toward her and shaking my head. "I'm not sure if I'll be able to pay you back. Like ever."

"You'll pay her back," Debbie Dually said and appeared next to Jo Francis. "She is a secret keeper, and you can trust her. She's a loyal mother, and loyalty is important to her."

"You don't ever have to pay me back in cash." I wasn't sure what she was trying to say, but there was some meaning in her words, and I didn't know what that was… yet. She pushed it back toward me.

In cash? What did that mean? I didn't ask.

"Are you sure?" I asked, somewhat confused and conflicted.

"Don't push me. Take the money. Pay off the loan and treat my son well." She turned, and like one of her horses, she trotted out of the office.

Chapter Seventeen

The check was hot in my hand, and I was nervous just holding it. I'd never seen so much money in my life. I wished I could say I was so excited about the money Jo Francis had given me to get out of my financial business problem, but I was so stinking mad at Bea Allen Burns telling everyone in town about my issues that I wanted to get the check in the bank and start collecting back the clients that she stole.

There was no time like the present. It was killing me waiting for Jack Henry to text me what was going on, and if I'd gotten the time correct, he'd probably just drove into the Lexington city limits. There was plenty of time to head to the bank and make a few house visits to the Clarks, the Fenwicks, and Pastor Brown.

I knew Pastor Brown would be at the Normal Baptist Church, and it was along Main Street, so I decided to take a walk down there to see him and enjoy what was left of the bright sunny morning, since there was a gray cloud off in the distance, making me think rain was coming.

The sound of a moped whizzed behind me and started to slow. Before I turned around, I knew it was Granny. She slowed down beside me as I walked on the sidewalk going to the church.

The edges of her red hair stuck out from the leather skullcap motorcycle helmet, and her eyes were magnified from behind the driving goggles.

"Where are you going?" she asked me.

"I need to go see Pastor Brown about coming back to Eternal Slumber," I told her over the moped exhaust that sounded like it'd seen better days. "Mr. Peabody sure was good at getting me off those charges."

"I think I'm gonna tell him to get lost." Granny's toes barely hit the ground when she brought the moped to a stop. She turned it off and guided it to the curb, where she apparently wanted to keep talking to me.

"He's such a nice man," I whined, and for a split second, I thought about telling her about how crazy Doc Clyde seemed when he stopped me and how sweet Mr. Peabody was when he came to see me, then stopped myself as I truly listened to what Granny wanted.

"Him and Clyde are driving me bonkers. I don't know what these two think they're gonna get from me. I just want to be taken to supper a time or two during the month, nothing more than that." She shook a crooked finger at me. "They want someone to do their laundry, cleaning, and wait on them hand and foot, and Zula Fae Raines Payne ain't doing that for no man."

I loved how she referred to herself in third person.

"You can take a lesson from her." Debbie Dually had joined us.

I laughed. If Debbie only knew exactly how Granny really was about my life.

"Uh-oh." Granny snapped her finger in my face before she threw the palm of her hand on my forehead. "You got the trauma? I see that look in your eye."

"No, Granny." I inhaled deeply. "I'm fine. I was trying to wrap my head around you having men issues and what advice I could give you, but I'm at a loss for words."

"She's not going to have time for a man." Debbie Dually swished the feather around Granny, surrounding Granny in smoke.

I tried not to chuckle. If Granny knew that Debbie was doing this ritual to her and reading her, Granny would've had a fit and marched right on down to Pastor Brown for a full-body baptism.

"She's got a future ahead of her that will give her the power she needs to take care of so many people." Had Debbie's ghost lost her mind? Didn't she realize Granny was elderly and just fine running the Inn? "Her time will be limited to those close to her, and it's not fair to start a relationship that will need to be nurtured. They will only get hurt."

"Maybe you don't need anyone right now." I had to ask Debbie what she meant, so telling Granny her instincts were right was the plan. "We need to spend more time together."

"I'd love that, but I've got myself to take of right now. I'm headed to Girl's Best Friend to get some touch-up." She patted the skullcap when she talked about her hair color. "For some reason I'm feeling like I need to be ready for something. Something bigger." It was like she knew what Debbie had said. "Honey, you could use a little something." Her eyes drew up and down my body before she turned the key of the moped on and twisted the throttle, taking off in a rush.

"What was that about?" John Howard Lloyd scared me to death when he walked out of the alley between Eternal

Slumber and Pose and Relax Yoga Studio. "Zula looked to be in a hurry."

"John Howard, you scared me to death." I smiled. "You know Granny. She's always off getting into trouble somehow. "

Debbie took one look at John Howard and ghosted away, sending a slight chill along my legs.

"You okay, Emma Lee? If you're not, you let me know." John Howard had been acting awfully peculiar lately. Was the odd-job lifestyle getting to him? Was he getting ill?

"I'm doing fine. Are you?" I asked him.

"Just fine. It looks like it's about to storm." He glanced up to the sky.

"It does, so I better hurry up if I'm going to get my errands done. I'm going to stop by to see Pastor Brown, the Fenwicks, and the Clarks to see if they will come back to Eternal Slumber for all their burial needs now that I'm no longer a suspect." I pointed to him. "Gotta keep you and I employed."

"About that," John Howard started to say, but we got interrupted by the opening of the door at Pose and Relax.

"Emma Lee." Pastor Brown walked out with a yoga mat under his arm. "John Howard," he greeted us.

Shock and awe came over me. It was the first time I'd ever seen Pastor Brown in a pair of shorts and a T-shirt instead of his usual brown suit that was too small and hit at his wristbones. His thinning black hair wasn't combed over but slicked back.

"Oh my, hello." Mable Claire waddled out behind him. She still had on her usual jogger outfit and jiggled like she normally did. "Here you go, kids." She dug down in her pocket and handed me and John Howard a dime each. "Pastor, you ready to go?"

Mable Claire tucked her hand in Pastor Brown's elbow.

"You don't have to call me Pastor since…" He wasn't very good at whispering.

"Shh." Mable Claire was quick to shush him up and drag him past us.

"Ummm… Pastor Brown." I gave John Howard a quick wave bye and scurried up behind the two lovebirds. "I was actually walking down to the church to see you."

"Is something wrong, Emma Lee?" Mable Claire asked me, dropping her hand from the preacher. "Is Zula Fae okay?"

"Everything is great. In fact, I wanted to ask Pastor Brown if he'd come back to Eternal Slumber now that I'm no longer a suspect in Debbie Dually's murder." I looked between them, trying to see them as a couple, but couldn't picture it.

"Of course he will." Mable Claire winked at me. "Now if you'll excuse us, we've got a lunch date."

"That was weird," I muttered and headed back to the funeral home to get the hearse since I no longer had to walk down to the church.

It was none too soon either. The gray clouds opened up, and it was pouring. The rain wasn't going to put a damper on my spirits.

My first stop was the trailer park behind the town square where the Fenwicks lived. It was a nice trailer park. Everyone took care of their mobile homes. Most of them had little white picket fences around them. They all had carports, some turned into outdoor living spaces. When I noticed the Fenwicks' car wasn't in their usual parking spot in front of their home, I figured they weren't home. Instead of getting out into the pouring rain, I had one of those ideas that I'd call them later or maybe even stop by after I made the rest of my rounds, in hopes the rain would've stopped.

The Clarks lived out in the Triple Thorn neighborhood. The houses there were fancy with manicured lawns that were taken care of by lawn services. It was one of those areas with a homeowners' fee and a recreational area that consisted of a swimming pool and clubhouse.

The rain didn't stop me from being nosy, so I pulled the hearse right up in their double driveway and parked right next to one of their Mercedes.

From my car, I could see they were sitting inside of their all-weather room on the back of the house. Mr. Clark stood up and waved me over.

I got out of the car and tried to beat the rain, but the rain won and flattened my hair to my head.

"Let me get you a towel," Cissie Clark insisted and hurried into her house.

Mr. Clark had the remote control pointed to the TV and turned it off. He gestured for me to sit down on the love seat while he took a seat in one of the two La-Z-Boys.

"Me and Cissie sure do love it out here." He rocked back and forth. "To what do we owe the visit?"

"I wanted to come and apologize for what had taken place at Eternal Slumber." I took the towel from Cissie and ran it down my hair. "Debbie Dually and I were good friends. We did have a little disagreement the other day, but I didn't kill her, and I've been taken off the suspect list."

"That's good news." Cissie sat down in her recliner. She took the glasses off the TV tray next to her chair and picked up the crossword puzzle it looked like she'd been working on.

"Thank you. I also knew it was a hassle for you to change your arrangements to Burns Funeral, so I wanted to come out and ask you to consider coming back to Eternal Slumber." I sat there and watched as the two of them had some sort of eye dance with each other.

My phone buzzed a text in my pocket, and I knew it had to be Jack Henry. It took everything in my power not to check it.

"I'm willing to give a discount on the second burial." I knew if I sweetened the pot they might consider it. "I'll even throw in a free casket."

The negotiation might've sounded so gruesome, but it was part of the gig. Everyone wanted a deal.

"Well, Cissie?" Mr. Clark deferred the decision to his wife.

"Bea Allen sure is going to be mad. She was bound and determined to talk to us that day you had that fight." Cissie shook her head. "When Sheriff O'Neil came in to see you, Bea Allen told him you were having the awfullest argument with a client."

"Huh?" I felt my face contort in confusion.

"Bea Allen came in to see you while we were waiting for you to finish with that voodoo lady," Mr. Clark said, telling me something I didn't know. "That's when she asked if we were comfortable dealing with a funeral home who fought with their clients."

"Then when we saw that voodoo woman dead…" Cissie gulped.

"All that's water under the bridge," Mr. Clark said, putting us back on track about changing back to Eternal Slumber. "We didn't like how Bea Allen forced a sale on us, but there's no other funeral home in Sleepy Hollow to deal with."

The Clarks looked at each other.

"If the good Lord's willing, and the creek don't rise"— Cissie parted the curtains on the window next to her chair and looked out at the rain pelting down—"we'll be down there tomorrow to change back."

"Thank you so much." I stood up and walked over to shake each one of their hands. "I'm so glad to have you back. I'll take care of you just like I would my own granny."

There was a little bounce in my step the rain couldn't take away, and I couldn't wait until Bea Allen Burns heard about me taking about two of the three clients she stole.

"Why wait?" I asked myself, throwing the gear of the hearse in drive. "I'll go tell her myself."

Chapter Eighteen

The closer I got to Burns Funeral, the more nervous I got. I wasn't good at confronting people, and Granny wouldn't have approved of what I was doing, but I was tired of Bea Allen bullying me since she'd come back to Sleepy Hollow to take over Burns Funeral. O'Dell had had to step down from running it after he beat Granny in the mayoral election.

It was raining so hard, there was no hope for an umbrella, and when I pulled up to Burns, I noticed there was a Bobcat and backhoe in the back of the funeral home.

Were they remodeling? My gut sank as I thought about the business they were doing and I wasn't.

I waited a couple of minutes to see if the rain was going to die down in the slightest bit and checked my text from Jack Henry. The news wasn't good.

Natalia and Kent were back together. They'd reconnected the day before Debbie's murder and had left on an airplane for a getaway, leaving them with a solid alibi.

Burns Funeral Home was really no different from Eternal Slumber. They were both very old Victorian homes turned into funeral homes. The stately brick houses had wonderfully large rooms with big windows. The crown molding was something new buildings didn't have. The character added to the feel of the importance of a nice send-off. Just like Eternal Slumber, there was a large front porch with a fence. Burns had yellow brick and white trim, and Eternal Slumber had red brick with white trim. Both were beautiful, but the employees and owners were quite different.

Burns did have beautiful stained-glass windows throughout their funeral home that were original to the house. Eternal Slumber only had a couple.

They also had a grand staircase with gorgeous oriental carpeting covering each step when you walked in. Their offices were upstairs.

Burns also had a much better employee kitchen space, but I wasn't going to think about that now.

I was going to march in there and give Bea Allen Burns a piece of my mind as soon as I checked out the new addition for myself. And maybe gloat a little that she couldn't count on my clients to help pay for what looked to be a big addition.

Through the muddy mess of the rain, I could see shovels, rakes, wheelbarrows, and all sorts of digging tools. There was a small trailer in the back of the property with a faint light coming through the window.

"Bea Allen," I groaned and sloshed through the mud to go back there.

I swung the trailer door open.

"Bea…" I stepped up and looked inside, and no one was in there.

My eyes focused on the building plans laying on the drafting table.

"I'm going to see what's up her sleeve." I went in anyways and stood over the plans. "Oh no."

A mixture of anger and jealousy coursed through my veins when I noticed Bea Allen's plan was to turn Burns Funeral Home into one of those one-stop shop places like my sister Charlotte Rae had run in Lexington. You could go to a birthday party, baby shower, wedding, and funeral all in one day in one of these places. It was a hall for every occasion.

A venue that would for sure take Eternal Slumber down in a week.

"Maybe I shouldn't cash that check," I groaned so loud I didn't hear the door open.

"To what on earth do I owe the pleasure?" Bea Allen stood at the door, causing me to jump and knock the drafting table to where it tipped the plans right off onto the floor.

"I…" I was caught and bent down to grab the plans.

On my way back to standing, I noticed a plastic container with a skull and crossbones on it. For a second, time stopped.

Cyanide.

"I came by to tell you that I've got the files for the clients that switched to Burns." I made up something on the fly. Not only did I just find cyanide, but I realized Bea Allen had motive to kill me. Not Debbie.

I grabbed the plans and tried to put them back on the tilted table, but they fell back to the ground.

"Where are they?" She put her hand out.

"They are at the funeral home." I gestured to the door and scooted along the wall past her to get the heck out of there.

"Where are you going in such a rush? You've not even let me explain what my future plans are." An evil grin curled across her lips. Her eyes sparkled.

"I've got to go." I was happy to get to the door when she walked over to the plans that were still on the floor and picked them up.

The rain was torrential, and the wind was making it harder to walk.

"Emma Lee!" Bea Allen yelled my name. "Did you forget something?"

"What?" I covered my eyes to shield and try to see when I turned around.

Bea Allen was standing in the door with the bottle of cyanide in her hand.

"I guess you've figured out my little secret!" she screamed and took off running toward me.

A clap of lightning lit up the sky like a flashing bulb on a camera, blinding me for a second.

I crouched down when a big shovel swung toward me, and I braced myself for a full blow or to meet Debbie in the great beyond.

I heard a thud but didn't feel anything. Was this what getting killed was like?

"Here." I heard a deep voice distorted by the rain.

Slowly I opened my eyes and saw the outstretched hand of John Howard Lloyd.

"I've been trying to tell you that Bea Allen has been out to get you, but you keep avoiding me." He helped me to my feet, and we stood there over Bea Allen's unconscious body.

"Trevor," I said, my voice trembling after I'd gotten my wits about me and called his cell phone. "Bea Allen Burns killed Debbie Dually, and she just tried to kill me."

Within minutes and before Bea Allen even woke up, Sheriff Trevor O'Neil and the rest of the Sleepy Hollow Police Department had surrounded Burns Funeral Home, and they hauled Bea Allen off in cuffs.

"Emma Lee!" Jack Henry yelled my name from behind the police line that stretched all the way around Burns Funeral.

Fluggie Callahan and Granny, along with the rest of the Auxiliary women, were also on the other side of the tape, all trying to get my attention.

"I don't know how to thank you." I sat next to John Howard under a tent Trevor and the Sleepy Hollow Police

Department had set up for a staging area to be shielded from the rain.

"When I realized you were so busy trying to save the funeral home, I knew I had to follow you around to make sure all those mean things Bea Allen said about you didn't come true." John Howard had told Trevor how Bea Allen had been going around telling everyone how she had plans to be the only funeral home in town with the new expansion and services Burns Funeral Home was going to offer.

He also said he was pulling weeds outside of Eternal Slumber when he saw Bea Allen go in to see me but leave with the Clarks, though she'd gone back in after she told the Clarks she'd forgotten something. The Clarks confirmed to Trevor how Bea Allen had gone back into Eternal Slumber, which was when Trevor believed Bea Allen had slipped the cyanide into the tea, thinking the tea was meant for me.

"I grabbed a tea on the way out of the funeral home after I'd dropped the one in your office." Debbie's ghost started to remember what had happened to her.

She was standing there while Trevor was piecing together the puzzle of exactly how Debbie Dually, an innocent person, had been caught in the middle of Bea Allen's rage against me.

"I saw the Clarks walking along the sidewalk with Bea Allen when I was crossing the town square. The gazebo looked so inviting to sit and sip the tea while I waited for the sheriff to leave the funeral home so I could come back in to talk to you." Debbie's ghost started to fade.

"Debbie," I gasped as tears dripped down my cheeks while I watched her fade away.

One of the officers came up to Trevor and said, "Sir, we called David Dually. He's been informed that his mother's killer has confessed."

"She confessed?" I wiped my face with the back of my hand.

"Yes," Trevor confirmed. "You were her intended target like John Howard thought. I only wish he'd come to us instead of following you around. But I'm glad he was here to knock her out before you were her next victim."

Chapter Nineteen

With everything that'd gone on over the past week, spending some much-needed alone time with Jack Henry sounded like heaven. I'd spent the past couple of days with David Dually, who'd decided to go back to school and wait to explore his psychic abilities like his mother wanted him to. Before he left, he promised he'd keep in touch with me.

When Jack Henry called this morning to ask me to join him for a picnic lunch, I jumped at the chance. He had something to tell me. He claimed it was going to affect our future, making me a little sick to my stomach. I wasn't prepared to hear about him going back to the Kentucky State Police job since I'd gotten a little spoiled over the past week with him next to me.

Even with us busy trying to solve Debbie's murder, I didn't realize how much I'd missed him. I decided to put whatever it was he was going to tell me in the back of my head and enjoy what time we did have together.

There was a nice cool spell that'd ushered into Sleepy Hollow after the big rainstorm, and it was a perfect day to lie on a blanket and stare into his eyes.

The tension between us over him being placed on leave and trying to save Eternal Slumber from financial ruin just about did our relationship in.

My phone chirped with a text from Jack Henry.

I set aside all the new and re-signed-up preneed funeral arrangements paperwork that'd come in since Bea Allen had been hauled off to jail. I grabbed my phone off my desk to read his text. His message read how he was waiting for me near the gazebo across the street in the town square.

"All of this can wait," I said to myself and piled all the papers on top of each other before I headed to the bathroom to check my appearance.

It was good enough for a picnic. I had on a pair of jeans and a black tank top with black flip-flops. I grabbed my light pullover sweater from the wardrobe I had in the office. There were jackets, suits, and shoes in there for when I needed a quick outfit change for the business.

The sweater would be perfect for the cool breeze blowing through the holler.

Jack Henry was relaxing on the blanket on his back with his hands cradling the back of his head and his legs crossed. He was staring up at the sky.

"Hey, good-looking." I plopped down next to him and noticed the food was from Bella Vino's.

He rolled onto his side and propped up on his elbow.

"Hey, beautiful." He leaned in, and I bent down to meet him for a nice long kiss. "Since our lunch date got interrupted the other day, I thought I'd get takeout and enjoy it here."

"You sure are buttering me up for this news you're wanting to tell me," I said and lay down next to him. He rolled back on his back, and I rested my head on his chest. His heartbeat thudded in my ear. If I didn't know better, I'd think Jack Henry was nervous about telling me whatever it was.

"Emma Lee, I'm not going back to being a police officer," he said calmly, but his heart was nearly beating out of his chest. "I want us…"

I sat up. Was this the big moment? The big engagement? My mouth dried.

"You want us to what?" I licked my lips, trying to wet them.

"I think you and I are a great team." He sat up and took my hand. I started to sweat. "I think we need to go into business together."

Business? The married kind of business? The questions swirled into my head.

"I've been looking into becoming a private investigator, and I want you to join me. I've got so many contacts, and you've got your gift. The money is good. There's plenty of unsolved cases out there, and I think we'd make a great living at it." He grinned so big.

I blinked several times, trying to process the shift in what I thought he was going to say to what he actually did tell me.

"So...?" He wanted me to answer him. "Are we partners? Of course you still have the funeral home, and I'd do more than just murders. So we'd both have our own stuff too." His head pulled back. "You don't look like I thought you'd look. It means I won't be leaving Sleepy Hollow. Maybe I could use Charlotte's office until we found a new place." He shrugged. "I'm just talking out loud, but we can figure it out."

"I'm a little shocked." I forced a slow smile. "I never knew you wanted to be anything other than a cop."

"You didn't say you wanted to go into business." His eyes searched my face.

"I just wasn't expecting you to tell me this. I was thinking…"

"Thinking this?" He pulled a box from his pocket and opened it.

My heart fell into my toes when I looked at the diamond solitaire in the velvet box.

"Emma Lee Raines, will you marry me? Will you be my partner in life and in business?" He adjusted himself onto a bent knee.

I threw my arms around his neck and met his lips with mine, hoping this was enough of an answer.

I opened my eyes when I heard some rumblings coming from the Inn. Granny was standing next to the big oak tree where she kept her moped chained. By the looks of the leather biker cap on her head and large goggles over her eyes, she must've been going somewhere.

Mable Claire was next to her, fiddling with something. When Granny got on the moped, Mable Claire handed her something.

"Well? I want to hear your answer." Jack Henry pulled away from me, his arms still around my waist.

"Yes." Tears fell down my face as I watched him slip the ring on my finger. "Yes," I ugly-cried.

"My mom told me to tell you that you owe her grandkids." His words brought a smile to my face, knowing she was talking about the money she'd given me for the funeral home loan and this was going to be my payback.

"Lots and lots of them." I was all warm and fuzzy inside.

"Mayor Zula Fae Raines Payne is calling a council meeting today to be sworn in!" The sound of Granny's voice through a megaphone and the whiz of a moped caught our attention. "O'Dell Burns has resigned, and I've accepted the interim position and am calling a meeting for the official swearing in!" Granny's voice echoed throughout the square.

"Oh Lordy, Granny is mayor," I said in a shocked voice. I couldn't even imagine how this was going to make her even more cuckoo. Then I remembered Debbie reading Granny the other day when Granny had stopped me on the sidewalk in front of Pose and Relax. "This must've been what Debbie was talking about." I looked up at the sky and smiled.

"Zula!" Jack Henry waved over his head to try to get Granny's attention.

I grabbed his chin and pulled it to face me.

"I was going to tell her we are engaged, and she can start planning it for us," he joked, but this was no joke.

"Why don't we keep it to ourselves for a few?" I suggested, sealing it with a kiss.

About the Author

Tonya has written over 55 novels, all of which have graced numerous bestseller lists, including USA Today. Best known for stories charged with emotion and humor and filled with flawed characters, her novels have garnered reader praise and glowing critical reviews. She lives with her husband and a very spoiled rescue feline. Tonya grew up in the small southern Kentucky town of Nicholasville just like the characters in her books. Now that her four boys are grown men, Tonya writes full-time.

Visit Tonya:

Facebook at Author Tonya Kappes

https://www.facebook.com/authortonyakappes

Kappes Krew Street Team

https://www.facebook.com/groups/208579765929709/

Webpage

tonyakappes.com

Goodreads

https://www.goodreads.com/author/show/4423580.Tony

a_Kappes

Twitter

https://twitter.com/tonyakappes11

Pinterest

https://www.pinterest.com/tonyakappes/

For weekly updates and contests, sign up for Coffee Chat
with Tonya newsletter via her website or Facebook.

Also by Tonya Kappes

Magical Cures Mystery Series
A CHARMING CRIME
A CHARMING CURE
A CHARMING POTION (novella)
A CHARMING WISH
A CHARMING SPELL
A CHARMING MAGIC
A CHARMING SECRET
A CHARMING CHRISTMAS (novella)
A CHARMING FATALITY
A CHARMING DEATH (novella)
A CHARMING GHOST
A CHARMING HEX
A CHARMING VOODOO
A CHARMING CORPSE

A Camper and Criminals Cozy Mystery
BEACHES, BUNGALOWS, & BURGLARIES
DESERTS, DRIVERS, & DERELICTS
FORESTS, FISHING, & FORGERY
CHRISTMAS, CRIMINALS, & CAMPERS
MOTORHOMES, MAPS, & MURDER
CANYONS, CARAVANS, & CADAVERS
HITCHES, HIDEOUTS, & HOMICIDE

A Southern Cake Baker Series

GET WITCH or DIE TRYING

A Laurel London Mystery Series
CHECKERED CRIME
CHECKERED PAST
CHECKERED THIEF

A Divorced Diva Beading Mystery Series
A BEAD OF DOUBT SHORT STORY
STRUNG OUT TO DIE
CRIMPED TO DEATH

Olivia Davis Paranormal Mystery Series
SPLITSVILLE.COM
COLOR ME LOVE (novella)
COLOR ME A CRIME

Grandberry Falls Series
THE LADYBUG JINX
HAPPY NEW LIFE
A SUPERSTITIOUS CHRISTMAS (novella)
NEVER TELL YOUR DREAMS

Bluegrass Romance Series
GROOMING MR. RIGHT
TAMING MR. RIGHT

Women's Fiction
CARPE BREAD 'EM

Young Adult
TAG... YOU'RE IT

Copyright

Manufactured by Amazon.ca
Bolton, ON